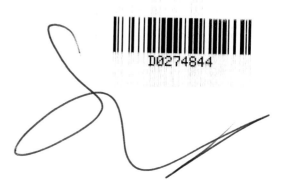

D0274844

About the Author

Pete Smith is a pianist by profession. He has worked with top class entertainers and musicians in many cities around the world.
He now resides on the island of Crete with his wife Anne and their adorable furry family.

LADY LUCK by Dennis Turner.
A poem dedicated to those who care when it matters.

Lost and all alone
Starving slowly and getting weak
It seems that nothing in this world is right for me
Everything so depressingly wrong
No hope, inside feel empty my days are long
Night time brings no comfort under the stars that shine
bright
Then out of the blue could hear gentle voices that call
Hands reached out to hold me I feel their warmth
Me a stray dog down and out without a name
They gave me home where I am safe
A garden with space to run and play
Meals that taste oh so good
Now I glisten in the bright sunlight
For me who was found abandoned in darkness on that
lonely night
LADY LUCK shone down on me
Now I have lots of love and a meaningful life.

Pete Smith

FURTHER ADVENTURES OF HARRY, POPPY, DIXIE AND ALFIE

Illustrations by Sylvia Leigh

AUSTIN MACAULEY
PUBLISHERS LTD.

A CIP catalogue record for this title is available from the British Library.

ISBN 9781786122131 (Paperback)
ISBN 9781786122148 (Hardback)
ISBN 9781786122155 (E-Book)

www.austinmacauley.com

First Published (2016)
Austin Macauley Publishers Ltd.
25 Canada Square
Canary Wharf
London
E14 5LQ

Acknowledgments

Again thanks to my dear Annie for her continual support
and enthusiasm about the sequel.
To Sylvia who stepped into the breach and came up with
the amazing illustrations.
To Susan for tackling my manuscript yet again.
To "Blondie" Sandie, my Fix-It mate.

CHAPTER 1

BREAKING NEWS

I mulled over the bad news that Bobby Badger has brought us, on what, until then, had been a most happy Christmas Day. With Ike and his gang seemingly out of the area, we'd had peace and quiet in the village. Old Ike and his two sons, the dreaded Feather Gang, had been terrorizing these parts for years, but with them gone, we had peace of mind. In fact, from the day of Ike's disappearance, we'd spent our days tearing around the countryside with all sorts of games and adventures, but now once again our safety was threatened. We'd have to make sure that all our friends knew of the impending danger. Calling the family together I said,

"Right, listen up guys. Tomorrow, being another holiday, might be a good time to let everyone know, especially since today they've all eaten too much and won't be going far. We'll set up a meeting for the day after, behind Matt's garage. We know he won't be there as he's still picking his olives." I paused and looked around. "Alfie," I continued, "you let Dottie and Red know. Poppy, you find the crows and the hedgehogs."

"What about me?" cried Dixie.

"You stay here Dix, with Mum and Dad – they're used to us taking ourselves off, but they'd worry if you go missing. Bobby, maybe you can let all the others know, except Billy and Angus. I'll get to them."

"Okay 'arry, will do," replied Bobby.

"Good man," I said. "Let's make it after breakfast, say about ten o'clock. Right, it's been a long day and I'm going to turn in."

"I think we all should," agreed Dixie. "Goodnight Bobby, see you at the meeting."

"Right-o Dixie. Night all," he said, and off he shuffled.

We went inside and left Mum and Dad in front of the TV. I had to laugh – they were watching a program about eagles, and the man was saying how beautiful they were. Certainly not the Feather Gang, I thought.

The following morning, Boxing Day, got off to a good start as we were given leftovers for breakfast – pieces of turkey, stuffing and all kinds of vegetables.

"Yum! Yum!" said Poppy, gulping it down. "Wish it was Christmas every day!"

"Watch your figure Pops," I laughed.

"Huh?" cried Poppy, "Me! I've noticed you're getting quite a paunch on you!"

"I must go along with that," agreed Alfie. "Mum and Dad should put you on a diet," he grinned.

"Now now children," called Dixie. "Let's not be cruel to one another."

"S'right Dix," I said. "I can take it. 'Sides, it's a treat from Mum and Dad, so let's all eat up and forget about diets for now. As the saying goes – 'We'll start tomorrow'."

We were always getting treats from Mum and Dad. Fact is, the four of us couldn't ask for a better life. We'd all been rescued at one time or another and had all the love and care in the world as far back as I could remember.

CHAPTER 2

FRIENDS OLD AND NEW

In my younger days, I lived together with Dixie in an apartment, outside of Agios Nikolaos. As a pup, I'd been found abandoned by the roadside and taken in by my now Mum and Dad. I'd instantly fallen in love with the beautiful Dixie, who had also been rescued a couple of years before. I wasn't the only one who loved her. There was Big Max, a large lumbering Labrador who lived a few blocks away and who was a frequent caller. Then there was Scruffy, a cheeky little terrier whom I had to keep my eye on. But as I grew I didn't get many arguments, we were all good friends and made many more. There was Mia who lived with Scruffy – he also fancied her, by the way. But then who didn't! With that beautiful black shiny coat and long eyelashes she was as pretty as a picture and all the guys fancied her.

We'd go romping on the beach where we made other friends – Henry the boxer, with his eccentric master, Stelios, the cocky wee terrier and the amazing seagull, Jonathan Livingstone.

Tragedy struck when Dixie got an eye disease and lost her sight. It was heart breaking, but she was very brave and we all helped her along. To this day, I have a small bell attached to my collar so she knows where I am at all times because she can hear me.

One day, Mum and Dad announced that it was time to move. They'd been building a house and now it was ready. On the day of the move, everybody came to say their goodbyes. Excited though we were, there were tears in our eyes as we drove off in hot pursuit of our furniture, precariously balanced on an open van.

We've now lived in our lovely home outside the village of Sfaka, in eastern Crete for more than a year. Our family has grown to four with the arrival of Alfie the cat, and Poppy the hunting dog. The four of us are inseparable and have lots of adventures together. Over the course of the year, we've made many new friends – Russell the crow and his two cousins Jeff and Martin, the two dogs Billy and Angus, Spikey the hedgehog, Bobby the badger and Dotty and Red, the brother and sister of our own Alfie. We all had one mission in common – to rid ourselves of the eagles, the dreaded Feather Gang, old one-eyed Ike and his two sons.

CHAPTER 3

ROUNDING UP THE GANG

After we'd eaten every morsel of our delicious Boxing Day breakfast, I gathered the gang around.

"Okay guys, listen up," I said. "You all know where to go and what to say – meet at Matt's garage ten o'clock tomorrow morning. Right – off you go!"

I'd given myself the toughest of assignments as I reckoned on being the fittest and strongest – well, they didn't call me Big Dog for nothing.

Billy and Angus lived on opposite sides of the village, so after saying goodbye to Dixie and telling her to hold the fort, I set off to see Billy first. He lived on the other side of Sfaka, and on arriving in the village, I couldn't believe how quiet it was. I reckoned that half the population was in church, whilst the others were still in bed, struggling with over-indulgence.

Billy saw me before I saw him.

"Hi Harry," he called. "Happy Christmas."

"And to you Billy," I answered. "Although it could have been happier. You've heard the news no doubt?"

"About the Feather Gang you mean?" he replied grimly. "Spoiled my Christmas dinner it did. Russell flew in and told me. Said he heard it from Bobby Badger."

"That's right, yes," I said. "So it's time to act. I've called a meeting behind your dad's garage tomorrow at ten. We're letting everyone know, so I'll see you there."

"You will indeed my friend," he said. "Give my love to the family. Where are you off to now?"

"To tell old Angus," I replied. "So I best be going."

"Old Angus?" he cried. "Blimey, that's miles from here! You must be the only one who's got any energy today! Me? I'm off for a kip!"

"Well enjoy," I laughed. "See you tomorrow."

And off I went – back through the village, which was still asleep, past our house, then up the steep climb to Angus' place. I spotted him in the garden – well, you couldn't miss that bright tartan collar – with the biggest bone that I've ever seen.

"Oy! Angus!" I shouted. "Where d'you nick that from?"

"Och laddie," he shouted back. "It was a wee present from the auld folk – and you keep yer paws off it!" he laughed. "Anyway, Happy Christmas Harry. Nice o' you to pop by."

"Well I wish I had better news for you. I expect that you've heard," I said grimly.

"Bad news is it? What bad news mon?" he cried.

"Old Ike and his gang are back in town with reinforcements," I replied.

Angus stamped a paw. "Och no! Not him again. I thought we were rid of him. What will we do laddie?"

"That's the reason I'm here," I replied. "I've called a meeting behind Matt's garage for tomorrow at ten. That okay with you?"

"Aye laddie – I would'nae miss it for the world," he smiled. "We'll figure out a way to get rid o'him once and for all."

"Good on yer Angus," I said. "Oh, by the way, did you have a nice Christmas dinner?"

His eyes lit up. "Did I?" he said "Ma mum Sylvia, being Scottish, had got hold of some haggis and black pudding. Ma dad Dimitri, did'nae care fer it, so I got his share. Delicious! Best meal 'ave had in years."

"Yuck!" I said, pulling a face. "Sounds revolting! See you tomorrow."

And away I ran.

Getting back to the house, I saw I was the last to arrive and Poppy sidled up to me.

"Careful," she whispered. "Dad's not very happy with you."

Glancing round, I could see by the stern look on his face that he wasn't indeed, a happy bunny.

"Where have you been Harry?" he shouted. "You've been gone for ages and you've kept us all waiting. We'd planned a trip in the car. Now get in! Let's get going!"

Oh no, I thought, not one of his famous trips in the car where we usually end up stranded, or lost, or both! Anyway, I gave him a few wags of my tail to show I was happy with the idea, and once we were all in, away we went.

"Oh dear," said a concerned Mum as we drove off. "I do wish I could have found Alfie. I hate going off not knowing where he is."

"He'll be all right," soothed Dad. "He'll be somewhere in the garden playing with his friends."

At that moment I caught a slight movement out of the corner of my eye. Under the passenger seat was Alfie looking up at me with a paw to his lips. "Shhhh!"

CHAPTER 4

A MUDDY ADVENTURE

"What are you doing?" demanded Poppy. "You know you're not supposed to come in the car."

"Well I'm fed up being left on my own every time you lot go for a ride. Anyway, why can't I come in the car?" he retorted.

"Because cats don't like it in cars!" I explained.

"Well this cat does!" shouted Alfie.

"Yes, well, I suppose you are different from other cats," Dixie conceded. "But goodness knows what Dad's going to say."

We'd been travelling for about half an hour when I realized the route we were taking.

"Hey guys," I said excitedly. "I do believe we're going to Long Beach. Yippee! That means swimming. Yea!"

"Isn't it a bit cold for swimming?" asked Poppy.

"Not for Big Dog it's not," explained Dixie. "When we were in our other home, the sea was at the bottom of the garden, and he used to swim every day – all year round. Besides," she continued, "the water's not cold here. When I lived in Cape Town, South Africa, I swam most days in the Atlantic Ocean. Now that's what you call cold!"

"Wow," said wide-eyed Poppy. "You lived in Africa?"

"Yes," replied Dixie. "I'll tell you about it one day."

Long Beach is where we used to go often in the summer. Mum and Dad would meet their friends there and we would swim, play games, and have lovely foodies in the cantina. Being winter, that wouldn't be open, but we'd still be in for a good time.

"You've never been to Long Beach, have you Pops?" I said. "You'll love it! Big beach to run around on, and plenty of bushes and trees to play. Then there is the sea, crystal clear it is."

"You know me Harry" explained Poppy. "Not much on swimming, not like you, but if it's not rough, maybe I'll try."

"Well it's generally flat as a pancake," I said.

"Oy!" wailed Alfie. "What about me then? I've not been there either!"

"You!" I said glaring. "You'll be lucky if Dad lets you out of the car."

"Of course he will," he answered.

"Oh, I don't know about that," said Dixie shaking her head. "You've not exactly been a good boy, have you?"

"But he'll have to let me out," insisted Alfie. "Besides anything else, there's the call of nature. Anyway, what you say doesn't make sense. First you say he doesn't want me in the car, now you say he doesn't want me **out** of the car. Na! That doesn't make sense!"

"Well, we'll see," I said. "But I wouldn't hold my breath."

Suddenly we were there – turning off the main road and down onto the beach and parking behind the deserted cantina. Mum and Dad jumped out of the car and opening our door Dad said,

"Right you guys, let's…Alfie!" he cried. "What are you doing here?"

Alfie purred, gave him a coy look and rubbed himself against Dad's hand.

"No wonder I couldn't find him," said Mum. "He must have been locked in."

"Locked in?" laughed Dad. "Hiding is more like it. Well, come on, but don't go wandering off and get lost."

Alfie grinned up at me and said, "See, clever sticks? Told you he'd let me out."

I had to laugh – Well, it's hard to get cross with Alfie.

The sea was perfectly calm and I was the first in. Aahh, I thought, this is the life! A few minutes later, Dad dived in and chased after me. Mum, however, stood at the water's edge declaring it was a bit chilly for her. Dad and I splashed around, then after a good swim, raced back to the shore. I saw Poppy jump in – and jump straight out again.

Shaking herself, she shouted "You're mad, the pair of you – it's freezing!"

I had to admit, that on getting out, it was a bit parky, the air temperature being what it was. So after a good shaking, I did a few lengths of fast running back and forth to the car. It wasn't long before the gang joined in, and leaving Mum and Dad playing a game of bats and ball, we scampered off to have some fun among the trees and bushes. I kept a beady eye on Alfie.

"Stay close," I advised. "There are a couple of large dogs not far away and I don't think they're too friendly."

"S'all right Harry," he laughed. "Remember, I can climb trees!"

And it was true! You can't believe how fast he could climb to the top. One day, we were having a game of hide and seek. Alfie was gone for ages – we just couldn't find him. We'd still be searching now but for a voice calling from above.

"Oy! You lot! D'yer give in?"

From that day onwards we made a rule that made tree climbing out of bounds. Well, it wasn't fair, was it? I mean, none of us could climb. Funny thing, that. I often tried when no one was looking, but I just got worn out jumping up and getting nowhere fast!

Since Poppy and Alfie didn't know the lie of the land, there was no hide and seek today, but we did have a wild game of tag until Mum called us for some lunch. Some yummy biscuits and a refreshing bowl of water – she never forgot, our Mum. After another dip and a romp around the beach, it was time to go.

"Come on," said Dad. "It's getting a bit chilly and I don't want to be driving in the dark."

"Blimey," I whispered. "You have enough trouble getting us home in daylight."

The gang giggled, nodding their heads. Mum held up her hand.

"Uh, uh," she said. "I'm not letting you in the car with all that sand and salt on you. Come on, there's a shower over there. Let's go!" And off she marched.

Now, there'd been a lot of rain recently and near the shower, it began to get muddy underfoot. Suddenly, Mum slipped, her feet left the ground and she came down with a squelch right in the mud! Covered in it she was.

"Ouch," she squealed. "That hurt!"

"Oh my, my! I bet it did," said Dad. "Here, grab my hand and I'll get you outta there."

"Can't quite reach," she said. "Can you get a little nearer?"

He moved a little closer, and it was then that he started doing a sorta wild, crazy dance as he tried desperately to keep to his feet. I had to admit that it was a brave try, but you could see what was to happen. And with a kind of "aaarrr" sound, he landed flat on his back, next to Mum. Well, I'm not one to laugh at other people's misfortunes, but it was Alfie who started me off. Honestly, I was really looking round wondering what to do, when I saw him lying on the ground, helpless with laughter, tears rolling down his cheeks. I just crumbled, and out of control, fell to the ground and slid into the mud, next to Mum and Dad.

Poppy being Poppy, who I may add, was also killing herself laughing, let out one "Tallyho!" and threw herself in to the mix.

"What's happening?" cried a concerned Dixie. "What's going on?"

This brought on a renewed bout of laughter from Alfie.

"Dix," he howled. "You're not going to believe this, but Mum and Dad, Poppy and Harry are lying in a mud bath and can't get up! Honestly Dix, I wish you could see this. They're like beetles on their backs trying to turn over, arms and legs kicking every which way. And aw, Dix, I can't stop laughing."

"Funny it may be Alfie, but what's going to happen?" asked a worried Dixie. "Come on Harry. Think of something."

"Well I'm trying Dix, but it's not easy when you're flat on your back sliding all over the place" I answered. "But hang on," I said looking around. "I've an idea."

I'd spotted some exposed roots from a nearby gum tree. Now, if I could grab it with my teeth... I wiggled my way towards them and with one final effort...Got it! Phew!

"Well done Harry," yelled Dad. "Hang on tight."

And he grabbed my tail (Oy! That's my tail. Ouch!) and slid his way past until he was able to grab the root and pull himself onto dry land. He then pulled me in and breaking off the root, threw it to Mum and in turn, pulled her in. Poppy was last to be rescued, but I don't think she'd have minded languishing there as she was having so much fun.

Standing there all bedraggled, wet and muddy brought another bout of laughter from Alfie. I suppose we did look a sight. Even Mum and Dad saw the funny side, pointing and laughing at Poppy and me.

"What do we all look like," giggled Mum.

"What indeed," answered Dad. "But you do all realise that we'll have to travel home like this. We dare not go near the shower and we can't wash it off in the sea as the towels are all wet. So let's get the show on the road."

One by one we squelched our way to the car.

As Dad opened the door to the car Alfie said "Harry! Poppy! You keep to that side away from Dix and me! Don't want to get your mud all over us."

Dad sat down and as he switched on the engine he groaned to Mum.

"Oh my poor car!"

"Yes," she said. "And you'll have a fine time tomorrow getting it clean, won't you my dear?"

See what I mean about our car trips ending in disaster? Although I couldn't help thinking that if Mum hadn't insisted on us taking a shower, we could have avoided the situation.

The ride back was uneventful apart from the moans and groans about being cold, wet and muddy. On arriving home, we were all given hot showers and scrubbed clean apart from Alfie who stood in the wings with a wide grin on his face. After being given our evening meal, Mum went down to watch some telly, and I called the gang outside for a parley.

"Okay guys," I said. "Tomorrow's a big day, so an early night will do us all good. I, for one, have had enough exercise for one day and feel utterly exhausted – I'll have a quick stroll round the garden, then get off to my basket."

"I'm with you there Harry," piped up Poppy.

"Here, here" agreed Dixie. "I'm tired out trying to look after you lot!"

"Alfie," I said, "I know you'll go out on the tiles as usual, but don't be too late – I want that brain of yours working tomorrow."

"Right on Harry," he answered. "I've had enough excitement to last me a week, so I'll give the tiles a miss tonight."

Laughing at that, we turned in for the night.

CHAPTER 5

PLANS IN THE MAKING

I opened my eyes in the morning and couldn't believe how I felt.

"Aw!" I complained. "I'm sore all over!"

"Funny you should say that," added Poppy. "I can hardly stand up!"

"Well it's your own fault," said Alfie as he came through the door. "Frolicking about in all that mud – funniest thing I've seen in years! But I must admit, Harry, you're a star the way you rescued Mum and Dad, not to mention Poppy."

"Talking about Mum and Dad," joined in Dixie, "I heard them saying they were stiff and full of bruises, and finding it hard to get out of bed."

"Well, I hope they make it soon," said Alfie. "I'm starving!"

"What's new?" laughed Poppy. "I don't know where you put it all, being such a little un!"

We took ourselves into the garden for our morning stroll. It was a nice winter's day – chilly but dry, with a few low clouds, but hopefully the rain would keep off for our meeting.

Returning to the house, our breakfast was waiting for us and, after gulping it down, it was time to be on our way. Alfie set a brisk pace and I shouted "Oy! Alf! Not so fast! My legs won't work!"

"Trouble is, Harry," he grinned, "you're getting old."

And laughing, he raced away.

Nearing Matt's place, I could tell there was a good turn out by the excited chatter that reached my ears. And turning the last bend, I was right – a large crowd greeted me, many of whom I didn't recognise.

"Happy Christmas all!" I shouted.

"Happy Christmas Harry," they shouted back.

Addressing them, I said, "Right, let's get down to it. We all know why we're here. Ike and his gang must be banished. So put your thinking caps on – I want some ideas."

It was then that I noticed a lone gull perched in a tree.

He smiled and said, "Hello Harry."

"By Jingo!" I spluttered. "Could it be?... It is! It's Jonathan Livingstone. What are you doing so far from home?"

"Well," he answered, "I heard through the grapevine that you had a problem with a certain gang, so I flew in to see if I could be of any assistance."

"Of course you will be," I said. "With your speed and agility, you'll give us a tremendous boost. Thank you. Thank you."

"Everybody!" I called. "Meet the famous Jonathan Livingstone Seagull."

A great cheer went up as he took a bow.

"Okay guys," I said. "Settle down... Let's get to the business at hand."

I noticed old Angus with his paw up.

"Angus, you've got something to say?" I asked.

"Aye, laddie," he said standing up. "We must remember that auld Ike is a canny bird and knows all the tricks. He's cunning and he might hear we're planning something, so I warn every one of you to be very careful." And he slowly sat down.

"Thank you Angus for those good words of advice," I said. "He's right guys – You must be on your guard at all times. So, any ideas?"

Bobby Badger had his paw up.

"Yes, Bobby," I asked pointing him out.

"Thanks 'arry – wot about diggin' a deep pit, lurin' them to it, surprising them, and pushin' them in? Details would need workin' out, but in principle, it could work. Wotcher fink?

"Nice one Bobby," I said. "Yes, we'll look at that. Russell, you have something?"

"Yes, Harry," he answered. "They can't swim. They're too heavy and their feathers get waterlogged. Again, they would have to be lured to the sea, but it could be done."

"Bravo Russell," I said. "That's good too. Yes, Poppy? What's your idea?"

"Well," she began, "this would take a lot of strength and someone would have to be a guinea pig..."

"Don't look at me!" interrupted Alfie. To which there was an outburst of laughter.

"A guinea pig," continued Poppy, as the laughter died down. "Then as they chase the bait to a chosen spot, we drop a net, trapping them under it. What do you think?"

"A bit difficult there Pops," I pointed out. "Where would we get a large enough net? And if we did and dropped it, what would we do with them? However, we won't throw it out – let's think about it."

"I agree with Poppy," came a little voice – and turning around, I saw the sweetest girl ever.

"And who might you be?" I asked.

"Harry, it's me Heidi – you found me in your garden as a pup."

"Oh my goodness! Oh my! Of course I remember. How could I ever forget that beautiful coat you have – the colour of cinnamon. And yes, Dad wanted to keep you but our house was full, so he asked his friends Rodger and Birgitta if they would care for you. How you have grown."

She smiled coyly and said, "It was a year ago Harry and I am happy to be here representing Kavousi."

A great cheer went up with that.

"Okay, anyone else? Yes Jon?"

"Why don't we take the fight to them? Find out where they nest and surprise them in their own backyard."

"Whoa there laddie!" cried Angus. "They're probably high in yon mountains which would require a heck of a climb. You and the crows can fly, but for the rest of us, it would be dangerous, especially this time of year with all the ice and snow up there."

There was a general murmur of agreement.

"I would agree," I said. "But there might be a way. Let's keep it in mind. Okay guys, I think that's enough for now, but if anybody has other ideas, you know where I am." And as the crowd started to move away, I turned to Jon. "Are you gonna stick around for a while?" I asked.

"Yes," he replied, "I think I will as there is something I want to discuss with you."

"Right then," I said. "Let's get back to the house."

"By the way," said Poppy turning to Heidi. "How did you get here?"

"I came with my Mum and Dad, who are just down the hill helping a friend pick olives. I best be getting back before I'm missed. But I will come whenever I can."

CHAPTER 6

JONATHAN'S VISIT

"So Jon – how's everything back at the old place?" I asked, once we were home.

"Pretty boring, Harry," he replied. "Mia and Scruffy have moved – though not far from here I've been told. Poor old Max is getting on and has a problem with his back legs, so I don't see a lot of him these days. And Stelios just disappeared! No my friend, the times are not the same, and that's what I wanted to talk to you about. I've come to a decision."

"Oh! And what's that?" I asked.

"I've decided to move out here."

"But that's fantastic!" I cried. "Wonderful! So when's it to be?"

"Almost immediately. One of the reasons I came today was to look for a suitable pad. I think I found one, but it's in your garden. Would that be okay?"

"Of course it would!" I said excitedly.

"No need to ask," joined in Poppy.

"You'll be more than welcome Jon," added Dixie.

"Man, oh man! We will have fun," smiled Alfie.

"That's great!" exclaimed Jon. "Thank you, guys. So, I'll be off now and see you in a couple of days."

"Don't you want to stay for something to eat?" I asked.

"Thank you, no – I want to be back before it's dark. 'sides, I'm not really into biscuits!" he laughed. "See yer guys."

"See yer Jon" shouted the gang, and off he went giving us one of his loop-de-loops as he soared into the sky.

"Wow!" said Poppy. "This village could become quite famous, what with Russell Crowe living here and now Jonathan Livingstone Seagull moving in."

"It's not Russell Crowe, Poppy," I corrected. "It's Russell the Crow."

"Yeah, yeah, I know," she responded. "But I like to think of him as Russell Crowe."

"Okay. Have it your way," I said. "Anyway, what'll we do with the rest of the day?"

"Since it's a nice day, why don't we take a walk down to Mochlos?" suggested Alfie. "I've heard there are a few interesting arrivals."

"Good idea Alf, we can have a swim."

"That'll be nice Harry" agreed Dixie. "But no mud baths, please!"

CHAPTER 7

THE MOCHLOS GANG

Mochlos is an enchanting village by the sea and Mum and Dad often go there for an evening. Going by car, it's a steep and winding road. Walking through the olive groves it's a lot quicker. Dad's done it twice – and got lost both times! Don't know how he managed that as it seems pretty straight forward to me. But whether he's walking or driving, he tends to get lost! Anyway, thirty minutes or so later we were by the sea on the outskirts of the village, where there was a sandy beach and Poppy suggested we go for a romp.

"Good idea," I said. "And I'll go for a swim. Who'll join me?"

There were no takers! I dove in alone whilst Dixie got her feet wet and Poppy and Alfie had a game of tag. Suddenly I heard my name being called, and looking round, my eyes nearly popped out of my head! Two girlfriends of Mum's, Karina and Sandrine, whom I'd often seen at the house, were each leading a donkey.

Both wearing brightly coloured straw hats, and bringing up the rear were two shaggy dogs.

"'Allo 'Arry!" shouted Sandrine in her French accent. "You enjoying your swim?"

"You bet," I thought.

"C'mon Sandrine," said Karina. "Let's join him. We've had a long hike." And stripping down to their costumes, they jumped in, whilst the rest of the gang made their own fun.

We'd met Karina's dog, Freia, before, when they'd been to the house.

"Hi Freia," I said. "Introduce us to your friends, won't you?"

"Hi Harry," she answered. "Well, that's Bouboulina, Sandrine's dog and the two donkeys are Leah and Naomi."

"Nice to meet you all," I said, and introduced my family.

"So you're the famous four," said Naomi. "Heard all about you, we have."

"Yes," joined in Leah, "and the problems you're having with those horrid eagles."

"Gosh!" I said, surprised. "How did you hear about that all the way down here?"

"Ah!" responded Bouboulina. "Russell ze crow flew by yesterday and tell us about ze 'orrible fings."

"Yes, and the meeting you were having this morning," said Freia. "How did it go?"

"Pretty well," I replied. "But it was a preliminary meet, and a lot of details still have to be worked out."

"Well, we're all here to help when needed," said Naomi. "Just give us a shout and we'll be there."

"That's great, thanks!" I said. "I'm sure you and Lea's strength will come in handy and of course we'll stay in touch. Now – what say we have a romp around before we go?" and off we raced. Well, some of us! The two donkeys weren't built for speed, but they enjoyed themselves hee-hawing and rolling in the sand, whilst the rest of us chased one another every which way.

"Whoa," I panted after a while. "That's it for me. A quick dip, then we must be off. Anyone join me?"

"Of course, mon ami," answered Bouboulina. "Allez Fria! Last one in is a…" and the three of us jumped in as one.

Back on dry land again, we said our goodbyes and headed for home.

"Cor," complained Alfie after a while. "I didn't realise it would be such a climb getting back. I'm fair pooped!"

"You can say that again!" said Pops.

"I said, I didn't…"

"All right! All right! Save your breath" I laughed. "Oh Alfie, forever the joker."

It was at that moment that I happened to look up, and there high in the heavens were four or five dots. I nudged Poppy.

"Hey Pops! D'you see what I see up there?" I asked.

"Gawd! Is it… is it them?" she stammered.

"It's them all right," I replied.

"Do you think they've seen us?" asked Alfie.

"Oh yes! They've seen us. Just letting us know they're there. Come!" I cried. "Best get going. Dixie, stick close – listen for my bell!"

"I'll do that," she replied. "Go! Go!"

We were all relieved when the house came into view.

"C'mon!" I shouted. "Last lap – race yer home!" And we tore through the last of the olive grove and down the driveway.

"Hello," said Dad, coming out of the house. "Had fun?"

'You'll never know how much' I thought as I charged inside for a welcome drink of water.

CHAPTER 8

A NEW ARRIVAL

The next few days were pretty uneventful. Dad took us on a couple of trips and managed not to get lost! Winter was closing in and the beach wasn't at all pleasant, not that the sea was that cold but the north wind was strong, making for big waves and I wasn't fond of getting water up my nose! No, not so pleasant! Then, by complete contrast, one morning the south wind took over. And I mean took over! It was ferocious! Six on the Beaufort scale, which is approximately 40-50 kilometers per hour. I mean, come on! It wasn't safe to venture out and when we had to, we tried to make it between gusts.

"Wow," gasped Poppy, "it's not safe out there."

"You're right," I said. "Be very careful outside."

One consolation was that Ike and his boys wouldn't try flying around in such conditions, so we could rest in peace – for now. We spent the time indoors discussing the various ideas that had been brought up at the meeting – that is, getting rid of the Feather Gang. At the end of the day, we more or less agreed on the idea of luring them into a net, although Alfie still didn't like the idea of being the bait!

On the third day, the wind stopped and it was a beautiful morning. As we romped in the garden, a familiar voice cried "Hiya guys!" and looking up, I saw Jon.

"Hey Jon," I beamed as he landed. "Good to see you." And seeing that he wasn't alone, I added, "Who's your lady friend?"

"Fellas," he replied, "meet Georgia, my new bride!"

"Hi Georgia," I yelled, "congratulations."

"Mazel tov!" added Alfie.

"Nice one," joined in Poppy.

Whilst Dixie, choking up, said, "Oh how lovely! A new bride!"

"Hello guys. Nice to meet you all, but my friends call me George," Georgia said.

"George Seagull?" smiled Alfie. "Sounds familiar."

"Take no notice of Alfie," I said. "Always the joker." And turning to Jon I asked, "So Jon, where are you planning on nesting?"

"Well," he replied, "I saw a nice spot just below the swimming hole – out of the wind and prying eyes if you know what I mean."

"Ah! That's near where Spikey and the Quill family live," I said. "You'll like them."

"Yes," said Poppy excitedly. "And close to Russell Crowe."

"Russell Crowe," swooned Georgia. "Russell Crowe lives here?"

"No! No! No!" I stamped my paw. "It's not Russell Crowe – it's a crow named Russell! How many times must I tell you?"

"Well," sighed Poppy. "He's lovely anyway."

"Doesn't hurt to dream, does it?" smiled Jon and quickly added, "George and I will get going now and get our new place shipshape. Will we see you later?"

"Well Jon," I replied. "We thought we'd go down to Mochlos again to see our new chums and find out if they've come up with anything regarding the problem."

"If we get finished, we'll join you later," said Jon.

"Yes," added Georgia. "I'd like to see Mochlos."

"Okay," I said. "It's easy enough to find – just fly due north to the harbour. You'll probably hear us before you see us," I quipped.

"We'll try and make it," said Jon. "It's a nice day for flying."

"Yes," I said thoughtfully, "that's what worried me! Be careful!"

CHAPTER 9

A CLOSE ENCOUNTER

Coming out of the house, Mum asked, "And what are you doing today, Aitch?" she often called me Aitch since the day their friend Fred called round one day and she corrected him as he said "'Allo 'Arry."

Dad said he was a cockney, whatever that is, and had a strange way of pronouncing his words – most of them in fact!

"It's not 'Arry," she scolded. "It's Harry with an (H)aitch."

Hence the nickname Aitch. See? She could have saved her breath though – he still calls me 'Arry!

After a good breakfast, we'd just got going when Russell appeared, with Martin and Jeff.

"Where are you guys off to?" he asked.

"We thought we'd take a run down to Mochlos" Alfie replied. "Got some new mates down there, thought we'd look them up."

"Want some company?" inquired Russell. "Me and the boys could do with some exercise, besides, it's good flying weather and we can keep an eye out for you, if you know what I mean."

"That'd be great," I said. "We'd feel a lot safer with you riding shotgun. Let's go."

We were about half way to Mochlos, I suppose, when Russell landed by my side looking grim.

"We've got company," he said.

"Where?" I cried looking around.

"There! Three o'clock and moving this way fast," he answered.

"Quick!" I ordered. "Everyone close up. Dixie, next to me!"

Just then, Ike and his sons landed some two metres in front of us.

"Hello Harry," he smirked. "Out for a stroll are we?"

I glared. "What do you want?" I demanded.

"I think you know what I want," staring at Alfie.

"Oh yes, you want Alfie. I heard he made a fool of you," I said.

"He did not!" screamed Ike. "He was just lucky, is all."

"Ha!" I laughed. "Not lucky – clever! Anyway I see you've only got your layabout sons with you. What happened to your other two hooligans who joined you?"

"Look behind you," he cackled.

And turning round there stood two of the most vicious battle-scarred eagles I have ever seen! And they were big! Very big! At that moment Dixie leaned over and whispered in my ear.

"Keep them talking. Help's on the way."

"How do you know?" I asked. "Are you sure?"

"Oh I'm sure all right. I can hear them moving this way and fast," she replied. "About four, I think."

Well I wouldn't question Dixie's hearing – she had the best pair of ears in the business, so turning to Ike I said, "Ugly brutes, aren't they?"

"But can they fight?" joined in Poppy.

"Well," smirked Ike, "we'll find out in a minute won't we?"

"And just how do you think you can get at Alfie?" I carried on.

"How?" laughed Ike. "How? Well there are five of us, which I think would be more than a match for you four."

"Four?" I grinned. "Now you look behind you!"

And there, not twenty metres away, and at full gallop were our friends from Mochlos – the two dogs Freia and Bouboulina, closely followed by Lea and Naomi the two donkeys.

"Attack!" shouted Naomi.

"Vive la France!" yelled Bouboulina.

Do you know, old Ike turned a whiter shade of pale.

"Aayyeee! Retreat!" he cried and they all took to the sky.

A great cheer went up and Alfie blew Ike a raspberry. "You haven't seen the last of us," shrieked Ike.

"Yeah, yeah!" called Poppy. "Come by any old time."

We watched them disappear in the distance, then turning to Naomi, I asked, "How did you find us?"

"Well, it's like this," she explained. "We were all out walking when we saw five eagles flying low in the sky. Suddenly, they separated – three going one way and two ze other. When they dived, we knew there was something afoot, decided to investigate and, well, 'ere we are," she concluded.

"Well," I said, "It was a timely intervention. Well done guys."

"Yes thank you, thank you," said Dixie. "I fear we were in a bit of a pickle."

"Nah mate," said Russell. "You'd have handled it, wouldn't you Alfie?"

"Course I would" grinned Alfie, winking. And as the tension was broken, we all burst out laughing.

"So, Friea" I began, "we were actually on our way to see you and discuss those ruffians, but I think we've had enough for one day."

"That's all right," answered Friea. "I know what you mean. We'll make it another day. Just send Russell down to give us the word."

"Will do, but it could be someone other than Russell. We've an old friend come to live near us – a very clever and special friend, Jonathan Livingstone Seagull and his new bride, George."

"What? George Seagull?" cried Friea, "sounds familiar."

"That's what I said!" shouted Alfie. "On T.V. probably?"

Smiling, I continued, "You'll love them and I guess they'll be coming your way a lot, to fish. Anyway, one of them will get a message to you. So, we must be on our way. Cheers."

"Goodbye all," said Dixie, "and thank you for your help."

"Yeah! Good on yer mate," called Russell. "See yer."

As we headed for home, Jon and George flew overhead.

"Hey," called Jon as they landed. "We were just on our way to find you."

"Well," I said. "We're back sooner than we intended."

And I proceeded to tell them what had happened.

"Blimey," said Jon grimly when we'd finished. "These eagles really are a menace aren't they? Something has to be done and done quickly."

"Yeah," I replied, "we're working on it. Maybe you and George can give it some thought. As for now, we've had enough for one day. Oh, by the way, how's the new home coming along?"

"Just fine," answered George. "Hard work, but we're getting there."

"That's nice," said Dixie. "You can tell us all about it tomorrow. Right now, please excuse us. We must be going."

And saying our goodbyes, we set off for home. We were all shattered by the time we were there. Dad was just driving up as we arrived.

"Hello, you lot," he called. "Had fun?"

'I wouldn't exactly call it fun Dad', I thought, as we went inside.

CHAPTER 10

A MOUSE'S TALE

Something strange happened that evening. Well, maybe not strange, but certainly different. We had a family of mice living in the house! Now this didn't worry us as we bumped into them from time to time and became friends over a period. Although we knew that they should really be living outside in the garden or somewhere other than inside. At the same time, the garden was fraught with danger and for that reason we were happy that they lived in the safety of the house. I say we were happy – Mum and Dad weren't! Mum said that a mouse didn't belong in the house and that we'd have to get rid of it. Yes – it! They thought that there was only one mouse and we knew why – Father Mouse had instructed the family to stay out of sight whenever Mum and Dad were around. But the little boy liked living dangerously and loved exploring and disregarding his father's wishes, he left their nest one evening and had been seen. So, Dad decided to set a trap – not one of those things that harmed the poor thing but a sorta' cage, with a tasty morsel inside, so that when it was moved, the door shut, trapping the unsuspecting mouse inside. Well Dad set the trap but it was as if the mice knew and nobody saw them for a few days. Dad tried everything from cheese to bacon, but nothing! Dad said he thought the mouse had gone, but Mum said no as she'd see signs that he was still here. Then someone told Dad to forget about savory things and try something sweet. So he put a raisin inside and bingo! We all heard the snap of the cage door in the early hours of the morning and rushed to investigate. Sure enough there was the youngster inside sobbing his heart out.

"Help! Get me out of here!" he cried.

But try as we may, there was no way we could get the door open. It seemed to be on a very strong spring. Looking at the mouse, I said,

"Look, try and relax – after all, you're safe in there. We'll try to come up with something. Stay calm."

But there was nothing much we could do, for as soon as Mum and Dad got up and saw the trap sprung, they couldn't wait to take it out and release the mouse – at a distance. I heard Dad say that it was no good letting him go in the garden, because he'd just come back inside. No sir! You had to go at least five kilometres away. So they decided on the next village, Lastros. Dad said it was a suitable place as there was plenty of cover there. Many pine trees – mice love pine cones he said. Do they? I thought. Very indigestible I would think. Anyway, rushing their breakfast, they set off with the cage in tow and the mouse inside wide eyed and terrified.

It wasn't long after they'd gone that Father Mouse came from behind the sofa, looking distraught. We'd been sitting there watching telly. Mum and Dad always left the box on for us to watch.

"Where have they taken my boy?" cried a frantic Father Mouse. "My wife's beside herself. If I told that boy once, I told him a hundred times – 'keep out of trouble!'"

"The eleventh commandment," chirped Alfie. "Don't get caught!"

"Shut it Alfie!"

"Listen up Mr. Mouse," I said. "We'll think of something – the gang's never let anybody down yet. For now, you should be with your family. Don't worry; we'll come up with an idea."

Easier said than done, I thought, as Mr. Mouse trudged off.

"This won't be easy," said Poppy.

"No, it won't," I agreed. "So let's put our thinking caps on."

"But I haven't…" began Alfie.

"Don't start!" I yelled.

Apart from dropping the young mouse off, Mum and Dad had gone shopping and didn't get back 'til past midday. They talked of the mouse, how he'd skipped away into the long grass after his release and Mum said she thought he'd be safe. We hadn't come up with a solution and Dixie suggested we ask our friends what they thought. It turned out to be a good idea, for do you know who came up with a plan? Jonathan's wife George! We hadn't seen much of them lately as they spent most of their time fishing and swimming in Mochlos.

"I don't think there's much point in trying to find him, then bringing him back here, where chances are he'll get caught again," she stated, on hearing of our dilemma. "Your best bet would be to take the family to him. You know approximately where he is and someone would have seen a mouse stranger in town."

"It's a good idea," I said hesitantly. "But it's an awful long way for the mouse family to go with their short little legs."

"Yes," said an excited Dixie. "But you and Pops have got long legs!"

"What d'yer mean?" asked Poppy. "We've got long le…"

"Give them a piggy back!" shouted an enthusiastic Alfie. "They're very small and won't weigh a thing."

"Gosh! That's it!" I said. "How many are they?"

"Four, I think," answered Dixie. "Mum, dad, and the two girls."

"Right," I said. "I'll take three and Pops, you'll handle one."

"Okay," answered Poppy. "But I'm sure I could manage two."

"Thanks Pops, but I've got thick hair that they can hold on to," I pointed out. "And just one would be comfortable on your collar."

"Yes," agreed Poppy. "I see what you mean. My short hair would be hard to hold on to."

"So," I said. "It's a bit late to do anything today. Dixie, see if you can find Mr. Mouse and tell him our plan. If he's good with it, we'll set off first thing in the morning."

"Right you are Harry," said Dixie. "I think I know where he'll be."

That night, it was impossible to sleep, although Dixie had found and told Mr. Mouse of our plan, the rest of the family sobbed all night. During the dark hours, Dixie went to them two or three times with soothing words of comfort. But it was to no avail. They were heartbroken. I must have dozed off in the early hours and I dreamed that I was in a race with Dad on my back. As we crossed the finishing line ahead of everyone, the crowd was chanting "Harry! Harry! Harry!"

It wasn't a dream. Voices were calling me. I opened one eye and there were four mice looking at me.

"Harry! Harry! Wake up! Can we go, Harry?"

"What? What? Go? Go where?" I stammered as I slowly woke up. Then I remembered – the mission for today.

"Good heavens," I said. "What's the time?"

"Well," answered Mrs. Mouse. "It's a bit early but…"

"Listen Mrs. Mouse," interrupted Poppy. "No one is going anywhere until we've all had a hearty breakfast. We've a long trip ahead of us and we'll need all our strength."

"She's right," I said. "So go and eat, grab your belongings and we'll call you when we're ready."

"Yes I suppose you're right," sighed Mrs. Mouse. "But the waiting is killing me."

They'd woken us up very early because Mum and Dad didn't stir for another hour and it was a further hour before we got breakfast. I saw Mrs. Mouse peering round the sofa more than once, most concerned. But at last, we were ready to go. Dixie called the mouse family and they scampered out clutching their belongings.

"Okay guys, listen!" I said. "First of all Alfie and Dixie, you stay here."

"But Harry…" started Alfie.

"No buts, Alfie," I said sternly. "We're not going to be hanging about. 'Sides, I want you to keep Dix company. We'll tell you all when we return."

Sulking a little Alfie said, "Oh, all right then, but you be careful – the pair of you watch for Ike and his gang."

"You bet," I said. "But you've just given me an idea, go find Jonathan or Russell – explain the situation and see if either of them can ride shotgun."

"Good thinking," he said as he ran off.

"Right, you lot gather round. We'll be off in a few minutes so here's what I want you to do. Pops and I will lie down and Mr. Mouse, you climb aboard Pops and hang on to her collar. The rest of you, on me and grab my ruff, my collar, or whatever. Get comfy and hang on tight. We're going to be moving fast."

At that moment Alfie appeared.

"Look who's here?" he grinned. "The whole crew!"

And sure enough there was Russell with his two cousins, Jeff and Martin, as well as Jon and George.

"Hey fellas," I said. "I must admit I feel safer with you lot joining us. Right, up you get mice and let's head for the hills!

With Alfie sure that they were all aboard, we set off.

"Oh! Do be careful," called Dixie. "And return safely. God speed."

CHAPTER 11

THE JOURNEY

The first part of the journey was downhill and we literally flew. Poppy galloped beside me and out of the corner of my eye, I could see a petrified Mr. Mouse hanging on for dear life. I on the other hand, could hear squeals of delight coming from above.

Poppy drew closer and yelled, "Mother has got her eyes tightly shut, but you should see the two girls – flying along horizontally and hanging on by one hand!"

"Well, tell them not to be reckless!" I shouted. "If we hit a bump or something and they fall off, we'll never find them in this terrain."

Gradually the land flattened out and turned into a steep climb and we slowed to a walk.

"Phew!" panted Poppy. "I enjoyed the run, but this is no fun."

"You're right," I agreed. "Take your time – we've still a way to go."

"How far?" asked an agitated Mr. Mouse.

"Well," I said, "we're about half way, so be patient – we'll get you there."

And so it was that after what seemed an age, an excited Russell flew down to say Lastros was just ahead and, yes, there were the group of fir trees where Mum and Dad had dropped the young mouse.

"Right you lot," I panted dropping to the ground. "Down you get and keep together!"

I saw Mr. Mouse clamber down from Poppy, shaking all over.

"Oh my word," he stammered. "I'll never be the same again!"

"Wow! That was fun," chorused the two girls.

"I'm glad you think so," glared Mrs. Mouse. "What a scary experience!"

"Hi," greeted Jon, landing among us. "Listen, the rest of the crew have spread out looking for anyone who might have seen Junior. I suggest you wait here and we'll bring you news as soon as we have some. Right! I'm off." And so saying, he took to the air.

"I do hope they have some luck," said a worried Mrs. Mouse.

"Don't you worry Mama," I answered. "If anybody can find Junior, it's Russell and his crew."

"Oh what I wouldn't give for a nice bowl of water," was all Poppy said.

"Yes," I replied, "me too, but we'll just have to be patient. We mustn't go wandering around in this strange place."

"You hear that girls?" shouted Mr. Mouse, noticing the girls chasing one another around the trees. "Stay close."

"We will Dad," they called. "Don't worry."

At that moment, an excited Russell and his crew landed.

"Right, listen up," he said. "We may have some good news. Among the few creatures that were around, we met an old hare and quite informative he was. Said he was always on the alert – had to be, he said, as there was often the odd man with a gun, and pretty trigger-happy they were too. Anyway, only this morning, he saw a mouse that he didn't recognise from round here. Tried to make conversation, but he kept himself to himself. Just nose to the ground – rummaging for food. Anyway he did give us a description; about two inches high and four inches long, brown eyes, brown hair, large ears and a long tail."

"Sounds like any old mouse," mused Poppy.

"Yes," agreed Russell. "But the hare noticed that he had a big chunk of fur missing near his neck."

"Yes! Yes!" cried an excited Mrs. Mouse. "That's him! That's him! One day when we were playing outside, he got caught on a nail sticking out of the fence and left some fur on the fence as he pulled away!"

"So it must be him," said Russell. "Well, on the off chance that it was him, I asked the hare that if he saw him again, to tell him his family would be waiting for him by the fir trees."

"Well done Russell," cried Poppy.

"Yes, well done indeed," I agreed. "We'll wait here, but it'd probably be a good idea if you carry on looking Russell, just in case it wasn't him."

Russell needed no second asking and with a whoosh, he was gone.

"Oh dear," sobbed Mrs. Mouse. "I wonder if it was him."

"Don't worry my dear," soothed Mr. Mouse. "I have a good feeling about this. Just hang in there."

The two girls continued their chase whilst Mum and Dad paced up and down. Poppy and I just lay with our tongues lolling out, dozing off and dreaming of a cool bowl of water. Suddenly we were aroused from our reverie by a loud shout.

"Boo!" And leaping up, we saw Junior running with all his worth towards us. Well, you've never seen such a sight as Mum and Dad and the girls rushed to meet him. Amid squeals of delight, they embraced each other and danced around crying tears of joy.

"Oh my boy," cried Mrs. Mouse. "We thought we'd never see you again. Oh it's a miracle."

"Mum, Dad," sobbed Junior. "However did you find me?"

"Well," explained Mr. Mouse, "it's all thanks to Harry and the gang." And he proceeded to tell him the story of his rescue.

"But," I added, "as much as we helped, our thanks must go out to Mr. Hare for his awareness, without him it could have been a long hard search."

"Think nothing of it, dear boy," said Mr. Hare suddenly appearing from the long grass. "Only pleased to be of assistance."

"You've certainly been very kind," joined in Poppy. "By the way, we never did get your name."

"Henry," he replied proudly. "Henry Hare."

"Well Henry Hare," I told him. "We all owe you – big time."

"Thank you Harry – and don't worry about the family. I'll set them up and watch over them."

"That's wonderful of you Henry," cried Poppy. "Three cheers for Henry everybody!"

With the mouse family, Russell and his crew, who were perched in a nearby tree, and Poppy and I, the noise was deafening and several of the local creatures stopped by to see what the noise was all about.

When it had quieted down, I turned to the Mouse Family and said, "We'll have to be getting back. I want to get home before it gets dark. So we'll have to go now and leave you in the safe care of Henry. But we promise to come and see how you are."

"That would be lovely," said a tearful Mrs. Mouse. "But isn't it a bit far?"

"Don't you worry Mama, we'll bring Dixie and Alfie and make it a day out. Come on fellas – let's go."

And after much hugging, kissing and shaking of paws, we set off for home, with Russell and his crew leading the way. With no passengers to worry about, we made good time but it was almost dark before we arrived home. Alfie and Dixie were waiting for us and wanted to know all the details.

After explaining all, Dixie, who had been sobbing her heart out whilst listening said, "Oh! What a lovely ending – well done you two."

"Yes," I said, "it was quite an adventure. A lot of fun but I wouldn't want to do it every day!"

"No," agreed Alfie. "You must be worn out. Come – your dinner's waiting."

"Dinner!" said Poppy. "Who needs dinner? Where's the water?"

CHAPTER 12

TRIPTI MOUNTAINS

The following day, Dad announced that we were all going on a trip. 'Oh no!' I thought, here we go again. What's going to happen to us this time? Never a dull moment on one of Dad's trips! Anyway, it seems he'd arranged to meet Nicole and Albert, two of their dearest friends, for lunch. Now, we all knew Nicole as she came to yoga at the house every week and always brought us yummy biscuits.

"Have you got a map darling?" asked Mum.

"A map?" he asked, quite surprised. "I don't need a map. Easy to find."

'I've heard that before', I thought.

"You sure?" urged Mum. "Some of those roads up there are confusing."

"Trust me," he pleaded. "I'll get us there."

Alfie grinned as he whispered, "It's getting us back that worries me!"

That brought a giggle from the rest of us.

Poppy added, "I've just been thinking about what Mum said, 'up there'. What does she mean 'up there?'"

We were soon to find out.

After breakfast, Dad rounded us all up, saying, "C'mon guys, let's get going. It's a long drive." And we all piled into the car.

"Oh dear," cried Dixie. "I fear the worst!"

As we got going, Poppy said, "Yes folks, it's another miracle tour."

"How do you mean – miracle tour?" asked Dixie in earnest.

"I mean it'll be a miracle if we get there," answered Poppy and we nearly fell off the seat laughing.

"I wonder if it's snowing in the Tripti Mountains," mused Mum.

"Mmm, I wonder," answered Dad.

"Oh me gawd!" gasped Poppy. "The Tripti Mountains! That's eagle territory!"

"Yes," I said, alarmed. "And I'll bet you a bone to a biscuit the Feather Gang will be up there somewhere."

As we began our journey, I saw Jon and George flying by our side.

"Mind if we tag along?" asked Jon.

"Not at all," I replied. "But be careful, we're headed for eagle country."

"Right," he said, "thanks for that. We'll keep a sharp look out. See you there."

"Okay," I said, settling back in my seat.

"Aren't they taking a chance?" asked Poppy.

"What? You haven't seen Jon's flying skills," I replied. "Old Ike and his cronies won't get anywhere near him!"

After some thirty minutes or so we started to climb and we all felt the drop in the temperature.

"Ooo," shivered Dixie, "I'm getting cold."

"You're right Dix," said Poppy. "We're quite high now. In fact, I can see some snow."

"Snow? Snow?" asked Alfie. "What's snow?"

"It's very cold soft white stuff that falls from the sky," I explained. I'd only seen it once before from a distance. And that's how I liked it! In the distance!

Just then, Mum turned to Dad and said, "I think it's time we had the heater on, I'm getting cold."

"About time too" complained Poppy. "Me paw is turning blue!"

Up and up we went, through clouds which made it difficult to see. Dad stopped the car as we came to fork in the road. 'Now what?' I thought.

"Do we go left or right?" Dad mused.

"Oh no!" groaned Alfie. "He's done it again – we're lost!"

"Now, now," said Dixie softly. "Have some faith."

Mum said "I told you to bring a map, didn't I? Oh well, try going left." And she was right.

As Dad turned left, we broke out of the clouds and there was a small picturesque village.

"There they are!" shouted Mum. "I recognise their car."

As Dad stopped, we all piled out. Nicole and Albert came running to meet us and there were kisses and hugs all round.

"Hi guys," said Nicole addressing us. "Look what I've got for you." And she placed a heap of biscuits and goodies on the ground. Never forgot us. Lovely lady.

"Right you lot" Dad said. "Go and enjoy yourselves, but don't go getting lost."

As the four of them disappeared into the taverna, Jon and George landed in front of us.

"Hey you two!" I said. "Glad you made it."

"Good to see you," answered Jon. "But brrr! Isn't it cold?"

"Yes," added George. "Who'd want to come all the way up here for pleasure? Much prefer my warm nest."

"Ha! Ha!" we laughed.

"Yes you're right" agreed Poppy. "Do you know it's the first time Alfie's seen snow? What do you think Alfie?"

"It's freezing!" replied Alfie. "For you lot it's not so bad, but with my short legs, I keep getting buried!"

This brought another bout of laughter before Jon said, "You should learn to fly, then you wouldn't have a problem!"

"Maybe we all should," added Dixie. "Can't we try and get to a bit of shelter? I'm cold. Brrrr!"

"Over there!" shouted Poppy.

"Nice one Pops," I said, and we gingerly made our way to a small clearing. Once there I announced, "Right, we've got work to do. Let's do some asking around. Seen anybody?"

"Well," replied Alfie, "I saw what looked like a wise old bird outside the taverna. Maybe we should start there."

"Right – let's go," I said. "But be careful of the snow. Try to keep to our paw marks we made coming here."

Soon we were back at the taverna and I couldn't believe I hadn't noticed the beautiful bird, all colours of the rainbow. He was perched on a branch about six feet off the ground.

"Hello there," I called, when we were closer.

Looking down, he shouted "Avast there me hearties! What can I do for ye?"

"What did he say?" whispered Alfie.

"Shh Alfie," I replied sternly.

"Eh, hello" stammered Dixie. "Well we were hoping you might help us. Could you kindly answer one or two questions?"

"Fire away," he squawked. "Gimme a broadside!"

"What's he saying now? I mean I don't…"

"Shut up Alfie! It's just his way," I said and continuing I called, "Thanks, well we were wanting to find out about a gang of eagles. They're up to no good and causing mayhem in our village of Sfaka."

"Aye, I seen 'em," he answered grimly. "Ugly crew they are. But I don't have much to do with them. Stick to me ship I do – lot safer. In me younger days, I'd have taken a cutlass to 'em."

"I bet you would too," smiled Poppy. "So you can't help us?"

"Didn't say that, did I?" he said. "Go find Bessie Badger – been here abouts for years she has. Knows everything and everyone. What she don't know ain't worth knowing. Just follow the path behind the taverna for about a mile. Call her and she'll come running. She'll be itching to know what you're doing here."

"Well thank you," I said. "Eh, do you have a name?"

"Bojangles' me name," he replied. "Mr. Bo Jangles."

"Bojangles?" gasped Dixie. "Isn't that a famous name?"

"You better believe it!" replied Bo.

"Why Bo Jangles?" asked Alfie.

"Well, yer see matee, I loves dancing – and drinking when I gets the chance." Which made us all laugh.

"Anyway," he continued. "Me boss always has music on as you can hear and I dances up and down me perch – loves it I do! Now me name wasn't always Bojangles. It was Cap'n Morgan, owing as 'ow I came from a long line of seafarers. Anyway, some years ago, a group of tourists – you could tell by their accents – came in the taverna. There was this one little fella who was makin' everyone laugh – very dark fella – had a patch over his eye 'e did. Well, me boss puts on this music – one of me favorites it was and I starts dancing, see? Suddenly, this dark fella gets up, comes over and starts to dance with me, singing as well. When the music finished, the whole crowd stood up and clapped and clapped. One of them called out, 'You've got some competition Sammy – why, he's better than Mr. Bojangles.' From that day on, I was no longer Cap'n Morgan but Mr. Bojangles."

"What a lovely story," crooned Dixie.

"Here, here," we chorused.

"Well Mr. Bojangles," I said. "We've got to get going, but we'll see you when we get back."

"Arrr! Right you are," he replied. "God speed and a good wind at your back."

And we left him dancing up and down to the music.

"Oh! What a talent," swooned Georgia. "And such a lovely colourful plumage."

"S' ok I suppose," said Jon coolly and we had to laugh.

CHAPTER 13

BESSIE BADGER

After a while, we stopped in a clearing and I shouted,

"Bessie! Bessie Badger! Are you there?"

And almost immediately she emerged from the snow covered shrubs. I had to look twice, for she was the image of Bobby!

"I'm Bessie. 'Ow can I 'elp yer?"

"She speaks just like Bobby," whispered Alfie.

"It's like this," I began. "There's a gang of no good eagles causing us a lot of trouble in our village. Our plan is to find where they're holed up. We aim to end their reign of terror!"

"Well," said Bessie, "I know who yer mean. Rough, tough bunch they are but you'll never get to their aerie. It's way up there!" she pointed. "There's no way up 'cept to climb and you can't climb 'cos it's a sheer rock face and 'sides, this time of year it's made even more dangerous by ice and snow on it."

Looking up we could see what she meant.

"No way," said Alfie, staring up.

"Impossible," agreed Poppy.

"George and I could fly up there and have a look if you like," suggested Jon.

"Forget it Jon," I said. "No point. I'm afraid that plan's out the window."

"Oh dear" sniffed Dixie. "Back to the drawing board is it?"

"'Fraid so Dix," I said. "So Bessie, we'd better be getting back. Nice to have met you – Oh Bessie? A question I'm sure all of us are dying to ask you."

"Yes?" asked Bessie. "And what would that be?"

"Do you have a brother named Bobby?" blurted out Alfie.

"Blimey!" she said, her mouth dropping open. "Well, I did, but we were separated many years ago. Why do you ask? Do you know 'im? Is 'e alive?"

"Very much so," replied Poppy. "He lives near us in Sfaka – good friend of ours."

"Good 'eavens! What wonderful news," she said, the tears running down her cheeks. "I must see 'im"

"Of course you must," I said. "But it's a long hike for you Bessie but we'll work something out, don't you worry – be patient!"

"Oh I can't wait!" she sobbed. "Thank you, thank you."

With that she trotted back to her bushes, and we started back to the taverna.

"What an amazing coincidence," said Alfie.

"You can say that again," answered Poppy.

"I said, what an…"

"Shut up Alfie!"

CHAPTER 14

NEWS FOR BOBBY

The ride back in the car was like a monkey house at the zoo, with all the chattering going on, with Mum and Dad amazed at the antics of Bo Jangles who apparently had given them quite a show. We in the back, of course couldn't stop talking about Bessie Badger and were impatient to get home, find Bobby, and give him the news. It was so refreshing to chat about something other than the eagles, although the problem had to be faced, and the following morning, it would be first on the agenda.

Arriving home, we jumped from the car and were surprised to see Dotty and Red near the swimming hole. Rushing down to greet them, Alfie said:

"Wotsup?" with a worried look on his face.

"Nothing's up," smiled Red. "Just visiting is all."

"Yes," continued Dotty, "got here about an hour ago. You weren't here so we've been round seeing everyone else."

"That's nice," I said. "We were out for the day and boy, did we have an exciting time! Met a crazy bird who did a song and dance act, and would you believe, we bumped into Bobby Badger's long lost sister, Bessie!"

"You're kidding!" gasped an astonished Red. "Didn't know he had a sister."

"I suspect he didn't either," smiled Poppy. "They were separated many moons ago according to Bessie Badger."

"So," I added, "it's quite possible he wouldn't remember her. By the way, did you see him?"

"Why yes," said Dotty. "Right after we'd seen old Angus. He was making his way down this way so I s'pose he was going home."

"C'mon," I yelled, "we gotta go see him!"

"What's this all about?" asked Dotty.

"You'll see," smiled Alfie. "Let's go!" And we all raced away in the direction of his pad. Suddenly there was a shout from above. It was Jonathan.

"I've spotted him 'bout twenty yards to your left. Oy! Bobby!" he yelled. "Wait there!"

"Evening all," he said. "Wot's happening? Went to see yer earlier but you was all out. Nobody 'ome. Now you all come charging up, scaring the life out of me! Wot's going on??"

"Oh! We're sorry if we frightened you Bobby," said Dixie. "But we do have some exciting news for you."

"Go on," said Bobby, suspiciously.

"Does the name Bessie mean anything to you?" I asked.

"Bessie? Bessie?" he mused, paw on chin. "Nah, can't say it does. Can't fink of a Bess.... Wait a minute! I 'ad a sister years ago named Bessie. Got separated as did all the family. Why d'yer ask?"

"Because," smiled Alfie, "we've found her!"

"Yer wot! Yer found her? But 'ow would yer know it's the same Bessie?" he cried.

"Oh it's the same Bessie all right," I answered, "spitting image of you. Even walks and talks like you. Oh yes! It's the same Bessie all right."

"Caw! Love a duck!" he spluttered. "Bessie! Blimey! I can't believe it, must be thirty years or more. Where is she?"

"Now that's the thing," replied Poppy. "She's up there," she pointed, "in the Tripti Mountains and it's a long hard climb."

"Crikey," groaned Bobby. "How am I ever going to get up there? I must go and see her."

"Well now," said Jonathan, "Georgie and I can help you. It will still be a heck of a climb, but much shorter. When Harry and the gang went, it was by car and all round the world 'cos they had to keep to the road. But if you go as us birds go, it'll be half the distance. Follow us. We'll get you there."

"Wow, Jon, I couldn't ask you to do that," explained an emotional Bobby. "It would take you ages at my pace."

"Don't worry about it Bobby," said Georgie. "It will be our pleasure. Just let us know when you're ready to leave and we'll guide you there. You could find your way back again couldn't you? That is if you'd want to come back."

"Oh, I'll come back all right. Couldn't leave all me friends could I?" Then thinking hard about it, he added "Maybe I could convince Bessie to come back with me. Wouldn't that be something? Caw! Can't believe all this" cried Bobby.

"Well, just give us the word when you're ready to go," said Jonathan.

"Thanks you two," replied Bobby. "I owe you one. Give us time to get prepared. Can't get over all this." murmured a tearful Bobby, as he shuffled off.

"Oh what a lovely story," sniffed Dixie. "Makes me want to cry."

"Stop it Dix!" wailed Poppy. "You'll start us all off in a minute!"

"I agree," choked Alfie. "Let's get home!"

CHAPTER 15

A PLAN DEVELOPS

That night, we all slept well, probably due to the fresh air and excitement. Dixie was the first awake as she generally was.

"Oh! Did I have a lovely dream," she sighed, stretching.

"Was I in it?" asked Poppy.

"She said she had a lovely dream, Pops," quipped Alfie.

"Oh stop it, Alf," I said. "What was it about Dix?"

"You know, I can't remember now," she laughed.

Just then, Mum called us for breakfast.

"Come and get it," she called.

And we all darted through to the kitchen.

"That's my favorite dream" smiled Alfie. "Food!"

We all laughed as I added "Yeah! We all know that when it comes to food, you've got perfect pitch!"

Finishing up, we ran outside. It was a cloudless sky with no wind.

"It's a perfect day for flying guys, so keep a sharp lookout for bandits. So, what'll we do today gang?"

"Well, first of all I think we should see if Bobby's gone," suggested Poppy.

"Surely he wouldn't have gone so soon," said Alfie.

"Oh I don't know. He was dying to see Bessie," I said. "So I'll see if Jon and Georgie are there."

And we scampered off. There was no evidence of any of them so we concluded that they were on their way.

"Oh dear," cried Dixie. "I do hope they'll be all right."

"Don't worry Dix," I said. "They'll make it. So what's next?"

"Well, I thought it would be rather nice to go and see Old Angus," suggested Dixie. "We've not seen him for a while, and I miss him."

It took rather longer than we thought to get to his place as we bumped into several of our friends. First of all, it was the Quill Family out for a stroll.

"Hello guys," greeted Mr. Quill. "Nice to see you all. What's the word?"

"Hi guys," I replied. "Well, we're still pondering the problem of Ike and his gang, but we'll get there. Talking of which, there'll be a meeting in a couple of days – usual place. We'll let you know the exact date."

"Right on, Harry," answered Spikey. "We'll be there. Where you off to now?"

"We're going to see Angus," said Dixie. "We've not seen him for a while."

"There's a reason for that," explained Mrs. Quill. "He's had a bad cold. Stays inside. Seeing you lot will cheer him up no end."

"Oh dear," said Dixie. "We didn't know that. Poor boy."

"That's a shame," I added. "Come on then – let's get going."

"Give him our love!" shouted Mrs. Quill.

"Will do!" we shouted, scampering off.

Rounding the corner to Angus' house, Alfie said:

"He can't be that bad – there he is in the garden. Hi Angus," called Alfie and Angus, on seeing us, ran to meet us.

"Hello gang," he said. "Och, it's good to see yews."

"You too," replied Dixie. "How are you my dear? We heard you weren't very well."

"Och aye lassie," he explained. "But just a touch of the sniffles was all. I'm on the mend the noo. Anyway, I'm so glad yer called. Been thinking about our problem."

"Haven't we all," said Pops.

"Aye, well," continued Angus, "D'yer maybe remember one of the first meetings we had, when we all threw ideas around?"

"Remember it well," said Alfie.

"Aye well," continued Angus. "Somebody suggested luring them to a spot, then dropping a net over them."

"That was me" shouted Poppy excitedly.

"Aye, so it was," smiled Angus. "Well one of the objections to that idea, which you pointed out Harry, was that firstly, we'd have to find one, and secondly, it would be too heavy to handle. Am I right, Harry?"

"Yes," I replied. "But what's your point?"

"My point is," he answered, "that we have a net right here, in fact, five or six."

"How come?" asked an intrigued Poppy.

"Olive nets! They're olive nets. Ma dad uses them to collect his olives once a year. They're not half as heavy as fishing nets and what's more they're green so they'd be camouflaged and they're right on our doorstep, saving us a lot of huffing and puffing!"

"Wow!" exclaimed Alfie. "Your Scottish brain's been working overtime."

"Aye, laddie. There's more came out of Scotland than Robbie Burns!" grinned Angus, which brought hoots of laughter from the gang. "Anyway," continued Angus, "what d'yer think?"

"Well," I responded. "In principle it's great, and we've certainly got the numbers if we include our friends from Mochlos."

"Oh they'll come all right," said Alfie. "They've already had one run-in with Ike, and you bet they'll want to finish the job!"

"I think that's a very good idea," added Dixie, "but somewhat dangerous. We'll need to get everyone together sooner or later to discuss it."

"Okey dokey," I said. "Let's make it the day after tomorrow. Russell, can you fly down to Mochlos and let everybody know? We'll meet behind the church – that's about halfway. You good with that Russell? I'd ask Jonathan but he's away helping Bobby Badger."

"No, no! That's no problem. I'm on it." And with that, he took to the sky.

"Okay gang," I said. "Let's get off home. Mum and Dad will be getting worried. Good to see you, Angus, keep well."

"Aye, that I'll do laddie. See you in a couple o'days. Be off with yer now."

CHAPTER 16

FAMILY REUNION

The following day was spent running around letting our friends know what Angus had come up with and the subsequent meeting. Russell dropped by to say that he'd seen Bouboulina and company and they were excited about the gathering. Then we had to find the Quill family and tell them about the change of venue. This meant that because of the distance, they'd have to miss the meeting as it would be too far for them. Well, at their pace, it would have taken them a month of Sundays, wouldn't it! Anyway, although disappointed, I think they were relieved at being spared the journey, especially Father Quill. "But," said Spikey, "come what may, be sure we'll be there for the showdown."

Later in the day, George and Jon returned from their journey with Bobby.

"Wow!" exclaimed Jon. "What a trip! Poor old Bobby, such a climb for him and oh, so slow! I shouldn't complain and don't get me wrong, but it took us eight hours there and twenty minutes back. A couple of times we asked him if he wanted to turn back, but he was determined to get there and finally we did. I don't know who was the most exhausted! Remember we probably covered four times the distance, flying backwards and forwards to make sure Bobby was okay."

"Yes," added Georgie. "Phew! No more guided tours for me!"

"But did you meet Bessie?" insisted Alfie.

"Hang on, we're getting there," retorted Jon. "First let's tell you about Bojangles."

"You saw him?" shouted Dixie. "How wonderful!"

"Yes," answered Georgie. "We remembered the taverna, but you could hear the noise a mile away."

"It was lunchtime," continued Jon, "and pretty busy. There he was, Bojangles, dancing up and down for the customers.

"I shouted out 'Ahoy! Mr. Bojangles' and turning around he beamed, 'Avast me beauties! 'Tis good to see yer. What brings you back here so soon and who's that you've got with yer?' he asked pointing at Bobby and added, 'Looks just like Bessie.'

"It should!" said Georgie. "This is Bobby, Bessie's brother; we've brought him up here to be reunited after many years."

"Bessie's brother eh?" mused Bojangles. "Well, shiver me timbers! Didn't know she 'ad one. You'd best get going then. Caw! What a surprise she's going to get. Anyway, I must get back to me dancing. Matie over there bought me a dram so I'd best get to it. Caw! Maybe I'll give up me drink just to see her face. On second thoughts…" And with that he gave a hic and lurched into a kind of jig as the music blared out once again.

"I think he'd had more than one drink that morning," laughed Georgie.

"Did you get to see the two of them reunited?" asked Dixie.

"Well I'll tell you Dix," answered Jon. "After we left Bojangles, we made our way to the clearing as before, stopped, and called out for Bessie. Sure enough, within seconds, she came scurrying out of the bushes. Georgie and I perched in a tree and watched. Bobby shuffled forward.

"'Allo Bessie," he said.

"Oo's that then?" asked Bessie, hesitantly.

"It's me! Bobby, your brother," he cried.

"Bobby?" she gasped, "is it really you?"

"Yer luv, it's really me." And with that, they flew into each other's arms, and burst into tears."

"Oh! Stop it!" howled Poppy.

"I can't stand it," wailed Alfie. "What happened then?"

"I couldn't tell you," replied Jon. "It was so touching; we were both tearful and had to get out of there. Look! I'm starting again!"

"What a perfectly happy story, don't you think Harry?" sobbed Dixie.

I must say I was pretty choked up, but I didn't want to show it in front of the ladies, so I cleared my throat and said, "Well, eh, yes eh. Wonderful." Then fighting back the tears, I said in a faltering voice, "You two had better go and rest. We'll see you later and tell you what's been going on here."

It was indeed a wonderful story, but I couldn't help wondering if Bobby would ever come back.

CHAPTER 17

THE PLAN GROWS

We spent the rest of the day making sure that everyone knew of tomorrow's meeting – where it was and how to get there. After reflecting on the past couple of days' adventures with Bessie and Bobby, we made a pact there and then that if Bobby didn't return, we'd go visiting.

The following day was overcast with a lot of low cloud – very dangerous for us!

"Watch out for bandits suddenly appearing out of the clouds," warned Alfie.

"You're right Alfie," I agreed. "Dix, stick close to me. Listen for my bell."

"I'll be right by your side Harry," she answered.

There was a buzz of excitement in the air as we made our way to the church for the meeting. We'd met up with Billy, Red and Dotty. Georgie and Jon flew alongside Russell with his two cousins, Jeff and Martin in a tight formation. Angus wore what looked to be a new multicoloured coat and collar.

"Had to wear the clan's colours for the occasion," he said with pride. He added, "It's the Campbell tartan, yer know!"

A buzz there was, but I couldn't understand how us few would make so much noise. Looking around, I realised that many more had joined us on the march to the meeting. As we approached the church, the buzz turned into a wall of sound and a great cheer went up as we stepped before the crowd. I looked around, then slowly raised a paw for silence and as the noise faded, I began, "Friends..."

"Romans, countrymen," interrupted Alfie.

"Shut up Alfie," hissed Poppy.

"Friends," I continued. "It's great to see such a big turnout. Thank you all for coming. Many of you I don't know, but I do know that we're all here for one purpose – to find a solution to rid ourselves of the menace that is Ike and the Feather Gang!"

Another great cheer shook the air. I continued...

"For too long have they ruled with fear and intimidation. They have made their intentions clear by recruiting two others to their gang. The rough, tough Clanton Brothers. They mean to continue their rule of terror. Well, that's not going to happen."

There were shouts of agreement all round. I carried on above the noise.

"So we've come up with an idea to get rid of them once and for all."

And I proceeded to outline the plan, telling them of Angus' suggestion regarding the nets.

"But where do we put the nets?" shouted a rather stout hare.

"We hang them in the foliage," I replied. "Being green, they'll be well camouflaged. And they'll be in such a place where there's a clearing before the shrubs to give the eagles clear passage to fly into them."

"Great plan," called a rooster. "But how do we get them to fly into the nets?"

"Good question," I replied. "The answer is to lure them into the nets."

"And how are we going to do that?" enquired a goat.

"With something they couldn't resist," I answered.

"Or someone…" smiled Billy.

Everyone at some time had heard the story of Alfie and how he'd thwarted and embarrassed Ike and his gang. Now, all eyes turned to him.

"What you looking at me for?" he pleaded. It took a while for the penny to drop and then, "Wha… you don't mean…?" he spluttered. "Aw fellas! Come on! That's not fair! Why me?"

"Because," I said, "they hate you! You're like a red rag to a bull. You exposed them for what they are. Out and out bullies! No Alfie, they won't be able to resist you."

"But what if something goes wrong?" cried an anguished Alfie.

"Nothing's going to go wrong," I replied. "It'll be planned to the smallest detail. Besides we outnumber them by at least fifty to one."

"So what do you think Alfie?" asked a hesitant Dixie.

Once again all eyes turned to Alfie, who was staring at the ground. Slowly, he lifted his head, looked at the crowd, gave a brave smile, and yelled "I'll do it!"

The crowd went wild and someone shouted, "Three cheers for Alfie! Hip hip hurray! Hip hip hurray! Hip hip hurray!"

As the noise subsided, a wise old owl raised a wing and asked, "Wait a minute! What'll we do with them once they are snared?"

"Ah! Now," replied Naomi, "you leave that up to Leah and me."

"Yes?" I asked intrigued. "And what have you two in mind?"

"Something zat will put zem out of action for a very long time," answered Leah. And looking at their bulk, I had a pretty good idea of what they were thinking.

"Okey, dokey. We'll leave that up to you then," I smiled. "That just leaves us to find a suitable site for the ambush. So I ask all of you to scout around. We'll be off now to work out the finer details. Thank you all for coming and we'll be in touch soon."

There were a few "Yeahs", "Bravos" and "Good on ya mates." Several came up and shook my paw, one being Peter Rabbit who said, "Please let this work Harry."

"Oh, it'll work all right, don't you worry Pete. And once again we'll all be able to move around safely."

The walk home was uneventful, that is apart from Alfie's moaning and groaning.

"Be brave Alfie," soothed Dixie. "We'll all be there to help you."

"Thank you Dix, I know that," he answered. "But it doesn't stop the butterflies inside and me knees doing Alexander's Ragtime Band! I keep seeing those beasts looming down on me."

"Relax Alf," said Poppy. "It'll soon be over, and then you'll be a hero!"

"Yeah, well," he responded, "I don't want to be a dead hero!"

"Don't be silly Alfie," said Dixie. "Do you think we'd let anything happen to you? Just think of it as another adventure. Come on everyone. Let's get home and do some planning."

And with Alfie muttering about dangerous adventures, we set off on our last lap.

Arriving home, we all agreed that we were far too tired for any debating.

"Remember," I pointed out, "this exercise has to be precise, so we'll need clear minds. Let's sleep on it."

"Hear, hear," agreed Poppy.

"Sleep! Sleep? How do you expect me to sleep?" groaned Alfie.

"Would a crack on the head help?" quipped Poppy.

"Seriously Alfie," soothed Dixie. "You've had a very busy day. You'll sleep."

And so it was that soon after dinner, we were all in slumber land. I for one don't remember my head touching the basket.

CHAPTER 18

ANGUS' SOLUTION

The following morning, out for our stroll in the garden, Billy came into view down the drive, closely followed by Red and Dotty.

"Hi fellas," I called. "What's up?"

"Nothing special," replied Billy. "The family's gone out for the day, so we thought we'd come to see what you're up to."

"That's nice," I said. "Please join us. We're off to see old Angus. Find out where the nets are that he told us about. Then we'll take it from there." As I said this, Russell and Jon, who'd become good friends, landed in front of us.

"Hi fellas," cried Russell. "What's up?"

"Hi you two," I replied. "We're just off to see Angus. What are you up to?"

"We're flying around trying to find a suitable site for the ambush. We've seen a couple, but not sure if either of them is quite right."

"Well, keep looking," I said. "But remember, not too far from Angus' place. We don't want to be lugging the nets any great distance."

"Right you are," said Jon. "So we'll get going. Catch you later."

"See you guys," shouted Alfie as they took to the sky.

"Talking about the ambush," remarked Poppy, "Ike and his gang have been very quiet lately, haven't they?"

"Too quiet," I replied. "A bit worrying isn't it? Keep a sharp lookout guys. He's up to something! Stay close Dix, listen for my bell."

"Yes Harry," she replied. "Oh, won't I be glad when this is all over."

"So say all of us," agreed Billy. "So let's get this plan on the road."

We'd gone about halfway when we spotted Angus running towards us.

"Hi Angus," I shouted. "We're just on our way to see you."

"Aye, I ken," nodded Angus. "Russell and Jon flew by and told me and I couldn't wait for you. I've some exciting news! I think I've got it!"

"Well don't give it to me," laughed Alfie.

"Shut up Alfie," we chorused.

"What is it?" asked Dixie.

"The site!" he shouted. "The ambush site! It's right in front of our eyes!"

"Really," cried a surprised Poppy. "Come on then! Show us!"

And off he ran, with us close behind. As he stopped, he slowly raised a paw, pointed and cried excitedly, "There! Look there!"

And sure enough, right in front of the house, was a clear patch of land with dense undergrowth at the far end.

"And guess what? It's all situated in such a way that the eagles will have to fly directly into the setting sun, thus being blinded."

"It's perfect," exclaimed Poppy.

"Yes it is," I agreed.

"And look," added Angus, "the nets are kept in that shed yonder. So we're talking a distance of what – a hundred metres?"

"About that I would think," I said thoughtfully. 'With all of us plus the extra muscle from Mochlos, it shouldn't be a problem."

"May I make a point?" asked Dixie.

"Fire away Dix," I replied.

"Well, half our help have to come all the way from Mochlos. It's a very hard climb from there. It doesn't seem fair."

"Don't worry Dix," I said. "At the end of the day, they want to get this over with as much as we do. They'll not even think about the climb."

"He's right Dix," agreed Poppy. "If it were the other way round, would you worry?"

"Well I suppose not," answered Dixie thoughtfully. "But I can't help feeling sorry for them."

"Yes, I know Dix," piped up Alfie. "You're nice to everybody though, aren't you?"

"Well Alfie," she replied, "I try to be, but…"

"What about us?" A voice boomed and turning round, there stood Ike and his two sons. "Do you say nice things about us?"

CHAPTER 19

A NASTY SURPRISE

I couldn't believe it! It was frightening how they'd approached us that quietly. We must have been so engrossed in our plans and I wondered how much they'd heard?

"Well, well," I said, hiding my surprise. "If it isn't old One Eye."

"Now, now Harry," he responded, grinning. "Don't be nasty."

"Crikey!" retorted Poppy. "Look who's calling the kettle black."

I stared at him. "Where are your henchmen today?" I asked.

"Oh, they are around," he sneered. "Didn't think we'd need them today."

"Getting cocky in yer auld age are ye?" piped up Angus.

"Just confident, Jock," he replied.

"It's no Jock! It's Angus," he growled. "Dinnae get me started laddie!"

"Hold it Angus," I said. "Don't waste your breath on him. Ike, I suggest you get on your way." I added, "You're no match for us today."

"Yes Harry, we'll go along now, but our day will come," he said giving an evil grin. "And Alfie, watch your back!" And with that, they took to the sky, laughing and cackling as they went.

"Oh dear," sobbed Dixie as they disappeared. "They're certainly up to something. I just hope they didn't hear anything of our plan."

Alfie gave them one of his famous raspberries before saying, "Now, where were we?"

He grinned and we all laughed nervously as the tension was relieved.

"Well I for one don't feel like any more planning after that little lot," said Poppy.

"Nor I," agreed Alfie. "By the way, what did he mean 'watch your back'?"

"He means be very careful," I explained. "And that applies to all of us. Keep your eyes open at all times. Just be aware. Now, what say we all go down to the French beach for a swim?"

"Yeah!" was the response.

"That way," I added, "we can tell the guys all that's happened today. You coming, Angus?"

"No thanks laddie," he replied. "The water's a bit chilly for me."

"Oh come on Angus," I chaffed. "You should be used to cold water. What about all those deep, dark lochs we hear about in Scotland?"

"Never ever put me paw in any of them," he answered. "'Sides, there's nasty beasties in those waters."

"Did you ever see one Angus?" asked Dixie open mouthed.

"Only the boss's mother-in-law," he giggled. And laughing, we bounded down the hill for a swim.

CHAPTER 20

THE PLAN IS COMPLETE

The day turned out to be a bit of a disappointment really. The weather changed, the wind was whipping up the waves and the sea looked anything but inviting. None of our friends were to be seen and we guessed they were keeping warm indoors. To make matters worse, it started to rain.

"Can't believe this," remarked Poppy. "The sun was shining when we left home."

"Yeah, well," I said, "I'm not going to stand here and get wet. Come on. Let's get back."

"Aw, gee," moaned Alfie. "You mean we did this whole gig for nothing?"

"Well it could have been worse, you know," pointed out Dixie. "Old Ike could have had his henchmen with him and we could have been in trouble. We were very vulnerable coming down that hill, and..."

"'Allo, 'allo!" a voice interrupted. It belonged to Naomi coming into view. "Quickly! Come into our stall and get out of ze rain! Allez!"

We needed no further invitation and sprinted after her. It wasn't exactly a spacious stall and we literally had to push our way in. Leah was there as were the two dogs, Boubou and Freia.

"We were having a romp," explained Naomi, "when the rain came. Like you, we weren't far from here. Even so, we got a good soaking. Anyway, how are you guys?"

"Very grateful to you Naomi," answered Dixie, "and thankful to be out of the stormy weather."

"It is our pleasure, mon amie," said Leah. "We must 'elp our friends. Would you like something to eat?"

"No thanks," I said. "We had a good breakfast."

"'Sides, we're not really into carrots and hay," quipped Alfie, grinning.

"Ah but, 'ow bout a nice juicy apple?" asked Naomi.

"Now yer talking!" beamed Poppy.

As we munched on a nice Granny Smith apple, Boubou asked, "So, what's been 'appening?"

So we told them all how the plans were going and our latest confrontation with Ike.

"Sacre bleu!" shouted Bouboulina. "Will we never be rid of 'im?"

"Soon, I believe," I explained. "We're practically there but for one snag which I'm worried about."

"Oh? You didn't mention it before Harry," said a surprised Dixie.

"I was going to earlier Dix," I confessed. "But with all the excitement it slipped my mind."

"So tell us," said Poppy, "what's the snag?"

"The nets," I answered. "How to drop the nets over them when there's no place to hang them from. The site's great but for this."

"Uumm," buzzed the gang as everyone absorbed what I said.

"Hey!" shouted Poppy excitedly. "I think I've got it!"

"Well, don't give it to me!" shouted Alfie.

"Shut up, Alfie!" we cried as one.

"Listen!" continued Poppy. "Harry! Don't you remember? A few nights ago when we were all watching the telly? There was a programme on Africa and…"

"Yes! Yes!" yelled Alfie. "I remember it and…"

"That's right!" I interrupted excitedly. "I explained it to you Dixie. There was a game park where they were moving animals to another location. The people chased them into the nets where they became entangled. Dad said they were called buck."

"What? The people?" asked Alfie.

"No silly – the animals!" scolded Dixie.

"Oh you crazy cat," laughed Boubou. "Carry on 'Arry."

"Yes, anyway, the interesting part about it was that they didn't drop the nets. They were hanging vertically so that the buck ran into them, getting their legs and horns caught and they were trapped!"

"Wow Dix! You beaut!" shouted Russell who was perched on a rafter.

"Where d'you come from?" asked a surprised Alfie.

"Well mate, I was flying around trying to find somewhere out of the rain," he replied, "When I saw you lot trooping in here, so I just followed on."

"Well, it's good to see you. Carry on Dix."

"That's it!" replied Dixie.

"Ah! Not quite," Boubou said "'Oos going to chase them into ze net?"

"Nobody's going to chase zem -eh! – them, into the net," I said suddenly seeing the light. "They're going to chase someone into the net. That's it!"

"Yes, but who will they cha… Oh no! Come on fellas! Not me again!" yelled Alfie.

"Now, Alfie," said Dixie, "you promised. You said you'd be the bait."

"I know," said Alfie, "but I didn't know I had to run for my life!"

"Aw come on Alfie," I said, trying to put his mind at ease. "You can outrun them any time. And anyway, it'll be a short sprint – say, fifty metres tops, then safe behind the net."

"Are you sure the nets are well camouflaged?" asked Boubou. "They're not going to spot them, or us hiding in the bushes?"

"No," I said. "Because the whole thing has to be done late afternoon – sunset! As we all know, the sun sets in the west which is right behind Angus' house. Are you with me?"

"Yes! Yes!" exclaimed an excited Russell. "At the time of attack, the sun will be shining right in their eyes!"

"Exactly!" agreed Boubou. "Wizz ze glare, it will be 'ard to see anything."

"That's it!" I said, and added, "You know, I think the plan's complete. Anyone think of anything else? Any questions?"

"Yes, I've got one," piped up Freia. "Alfie, how's your sprinting?" This brought a burst of laughter from everyone.

"Don't you worry 'bout me," answered Alfie. "I'll take you on any time."

This brought on another round of laughter before I put up my paw for silence.

"Okay guys, since there are no questions, I assume we're all in favour of the plan?"

A great cheer went up, and in the confined space of the stall, it was quite deafening. When my ears stopped ringing, I looked around at the faces before me and said, seriously,

"I see no reason why we shouldn't make a date here and now. What d'yer think?"

"Yes, yes!" said Poppy.

"Why not?" added Boubou. "Sacre bleu!" she roared. "I can't wait to get my 'ands on zat buzzard!"

"Right then," I said. "Let's see, today's Monday. Let's make it Thursday. That should be plenty of notice for everybody. We'll all meet behind Angus' house 2 p.m. Thursday afternoon. That all right?"

"If, it's a nice day," stated Dixie seriously.

"Yes, if it's a nice day," I agreed. "But I think it will be. I heard Dad telling our Mum that the forecast was for good, clear weather after today."

"Fair dinkum, but you know how it can change at the snap of a claw," argued Russell.

"You are right Russell," said Dixie. "So let's do some extra special praying this week."

"Right," said Alfie. "And we don't want anyone doing a rain dance!"

"A rain dance?" inquired Poppy. "Where d'you get that from?"

"I heard," explained Alfie, "that in some places, they do a dance and it starts to rain."

"Then," argued Poppy, "if they have a rain dance, they must have a sun dance, mustn't they?"

"Well, I suppose they might…"

"All right you two," I laughed. "For now, no dancing. Just say our prayers and think positively! You two do go on."

"But I only wanted to…"

"Enough!" I cried. And then changing the subject I said, "Look it's stopped raining and the sun's out – a good omen. Who's for a swim?"

"Yea!" everyone shouted.

Then it was a mad rush for the door, on to the beach and a great splash as everyone jumped in as one – everyone that is, except Poppy and Russell. Even Dixie and the two donkeys, Leah and Naomi braved the water. Well, up to their necks, anyway!

"You're all mad!" shouted Poppy.

"I'm with you there Pops," agreed Russell as he perched himself on the sea wall. "Don't see anything wrong with a bit of dry land."

As I swam toward the beach, to my astonishment, I saw a bedraggled Alfie dragging himself out of the sea.

"Alfie!" I shouted amazed. "What are you doing in the water?"

"Oh Harry!" he spluttered. "In the excitement, I got carried away and jumped in with the rest of you. Never again!"

"Silly boy," I laughed as I helped him out. "Come and join us in a game and get dry."

"No thanks – I think I'll just lie down for a while. Ooff! I'll never be the same again."

And leaving him stretched out, I ran to join the others in a romp around the beach.

CHAPTER 21

A NERVY DAY

Having said our goodbyes, we set off for home although Alfie was finding it hard going with half his fur plastered to his body.

"You all right Alf?" I asked.

"I'll get there," he puffed. "But I'll never know what pleasure you lot get jumping into that cold wet stuff."

And amid howls of laughter, we continued on our way.

So that's it then, I thought. Plans made – date set. All we had to do was attach the nets to the bushes, undetected – the hardest part of the exercise – and have luck on our side. We had enough troops, with ground and air forces, but it had to go like clockwork.

That night, it was hard to sleep with things zooming through my mind. Would the nets be strong enough? Would Alfie be safe? Sure, he was fast, but so were the eagles and thinking of them, what were they up to? Were they making plans too? With all these thoughts going through my head, I must have dozed off, for the next thing, a paw was gently patting me.

"Harry, Harry. Wake up sleepy head." It was Alfie.

"Morning Alf," I yawned. "Oh, what a terrible night!"

"You, had a terrible night?" he said bleary eyed. "I spent the time swimming away from a thousand eagles. I'm fair pooped!"

"C'mon you lot," shouted Poppy coming in from the garden. "Rise and shine. It's a beaut day out there."

The day was spent getting the nets into position. It was exhausting work and seemed to take ages, but by mid-afternoon after much pulling and pushing, stretching and bending, and a lot of blood, sweat and tears, we'd completed the task.

"Wow! That was hard going," moaned Alfie.

"Whew! You can say that again," agreed Poppy.

"I said…" began Alfie.

"Shut up Alfie!" we shouted in unison, as we stretched out for a well-earned rest. We lay there for a while soaking up the late afternoon sun when Angus suddenly said,

"I wonder how Bobby Badger's getting on?"

"Good heavens," said Russell. "Whatever made you think of him?"

"Oh, I don't know," answered Angus. "I guess I just miss having him around."

"You're right," agreed Poppy, "a good friend."

"Aye," said Angus. "I wonder if we'll ever see him again?"

"Oh! I think so," I said. "Maybe later in the year when it's cooler. It's a long trek in this heat. Anyway, enough chatter for now. Let's inspect our handiwork and make sure the nets are well hidden."

We looked from all angles and everybody agreed it was a job well done.

"Great work fellas," I said. "I think we can call it a day. I'm tired. So let's get off home and meet here again tomorrow to run through the final routine."

And saying goodbye to Angus and the rest of the helpers, we made tracks.

"Boy, I can't wait to get my head down," said Poppy.

"Me too," agreed Alfie. "But after dinner of course," he laughed.

We all slept soundly that night, from all our hard work that day, I suppose.

"Caw!" said Alfie, stretching, "I can't believe it's morning already."

"Yes," agreed Poppy. "Only feels like a moment ago I shut my eyes."

"That's good," I said. "We need all the sleep and rest in preparation for the big day tomorrow. You all right, Dix?"

"Oh yes thank you," answered Dixie. "Slept like a log. Not even Dad's snoring kept me awake," she smiled.

"Well if you slept so well, how do you know he snored?" asked Alfie.

"Because Dad always snores," replied Poppy.

"Yes, but how do you know he snored last night?" insisted Alfie.

"All right, knock it off!" I said. "Let's just say Dad snored, but we didn't hear it because we all slept soundly."

"Here! Here!" agreed Dixie.

"Where? Where?" asked Alfie.

"There! There!" shouted Poppy, pointing her paw at our breakfast dishes and we all ran into the kitchen for our first meal of the day.

"That was scrumptious," said Alfie, licking his lips.

"Enjoy that, did you Alf?" asked Poppy.

"Did you ever know Alfie not to enjoy his food?" laughed Dixie.

"Well you must admit we get lovely foodies," I replied.

"Here! Here!" said Poppy.

"Where? Where?" smiled Alfie.

"Oh me gawd!" I groaned. "Don't start that again! Come, let's get out, looks like a beautiful day."

Apart from checking the nets and going over the plans, we all tried to relax, but with our nerves jangling at the thought of tomorrow, it wasn't easy. Jon and George decided to fly down to Mochlos to do a spot of fishing and to see if all of our allies were ready for the big day. Russell, Martin and Jeff flew west to see if there was any hostile movement but reported back that they saw no activity. The rest of us tried a game of tag but our hearts weren't in it, and we were all relieved when it was time to get home. Mum and Dad were by the swimming hole soaking up the last of the sun, and we just flopped down by their side.

"Good heavens!" exclaimed Mum. "It's not often that the whole family's together."

"No," replied Dad, "and they all look tired out. Wonder what they've been up to?"

'You wouldn't believe it', I thought!

After dinner, Mum and Dad switched on the box to watch the news which was full of heartbreak and bad news. Dad said that after thousands of years, still nobody knew how to behave. Mum agreed. After the news, we watched the sports news (Dad loves his sport) and then had a movie to watch. We took up our usual positions, namely Dix and Pops, who weren't into movies, curled up in their baskets, Alfie out on the tiles, and me sat between Mum and Dad hoping for something to take my mind off tomorrow. I wasn't disappointed as it was a thriller. But what I liked about it was that among all the car chases, explosions and general mayhem, our hero looked after his cat throughout and carried him about in a bag. Actually he didn't look unlike Alfie – the cat, that is! Yes, my kind of film.

CHAPTER 22

WILLIE

'This is it', I thought, as I awoke the following morning. The big day is here! Were we ready for it? We would soon find out. Looking round I was surprised to see that I was the only one still in my basket. I ran outside and saw a pensive looking trio.

"We couldn't sleep," explained Poppy. "So we came out for a stroll. You were snoring like a trooper, so we left you."

"Yes," added Alfie. "We figured that you will need all your strength for today."

"Oh my!" joined in Dixie. "I feel so nervous – my tummy's in a knot."

"Don't worry Dix," I said. "I think we're all feeling it. Come, let's eat and get the show on the road."

But as so often happens, fate was to intervene that day and turn all our plans upside down. As the world famous bird comic Woody Woodpecker once quipped, "If you want to make God laugh, tell him your plans!"

Well, our plans would soon be well and truly turned upside down. It began as we were about to leave for Angus' house. A great screeching noise filled the air, and looking up we saw Russell, one of his cousins Jeff, Jon and Georgia speeding toward us. And the noise! All chattering at once!

"Harry!" "Hold on!" "Wait up!" "You won't believe…"

"Whoa! Hold on!" I ordered as they landed before us. "One at a time fellas. Russell, what's up?"

"Well," started Russell, fighting to get his breath. "We were all going for a dip before work when suddenly, we saw something falling from the sky, then heard a thud. Naturally we turned to investigate. It wasn't far away but as you know, it's pretty thick with trees in that area, and it took a while to find anything interesting. But find it we did and guess what it was?"

We all stood there, mouths open listening transfixed and it took a second or two to register the question. Eventually I said,

"Tell me!"

"A young eagle!" they chorused.

There were cries of astonishment from the gang.

"I don't believe it!" said Poppy.

"Get away!" cried Alfie.

"My goodness!" whispered Dixie.

"Was he... dead?" I asked hesitantly.

"No! No!" replied Georgia. "Quite chirpy really. Dazed and bruised but chirpy."

"What did you do?" asked Dixie.

"Well, we approached him very carefully – he is one of the enemy after all – and asked him how he was. He said that he felt a bit battered but that he'd live."

"Gracious," said Dixie. "Poor thing."

"Lucky to be alive," added Alfie.

"What was he doing in these parts on his own anyway?" I continued.

"We did ask him that but he was rather reluctant to answer," replied Jon. "But we did get one thing out of him."

"And what was that?" I asked.

"Who he was," said Russell.

"And who is he?" we asked in unison.

"Hold on to your hats folks," grinned Georgia. "He's Ike's nephew!"

There was a collective gasp followed by several cries of astonishment.

"My giddy aunt!" said Alfie.

"'Pon my soul!" added Poppy.

"Oh my word!" joined in Dixie.

"Has this young fella got a name?" I asked.

"Yes," replied Jeff, "It's Willie."

"Willie is it?" I said. "Well we'd better go and find out what little Willie has to say for himself – if he's still there."

"Oh, he'll be there all right," remarked Russell. "He's a bit too bruised to go anywhere and besides, Martin stayed to keep an eye on him."

"Dix? You stay here! We'll be moving fast."

"All right Harry. Good luck."

"Thanks," I said. "Okay, let's go. Right, lead on, you guys!"

It wasn't far, but it was hard going as the foliage was pretty thick and we had a difficult time keeping Russell and his crew in sight. I was glad we'd left Dixie behind. However, Martin heard us coming and with the help of his voice, we came upon both he and young Willie.

"How's it going Martin?" I asked.

"Not too bad, I guess," he replied. "He hasn't said much, but he's moving about more freely."

"That's good," I said as I approached the young bird. "Hello there my boy," I began. "Do you know who I am?" I asked.

"Oh yes," he answered. "You're Harry, I recognise you from Uncle Ike's description. He talks about you all the time."

"Not too nicely, I would think," I said sternly.

"Well he's not fond of you, that's for sure. But he admires you and your gang in many ways," stated Willie looking round at Poppy and Alfie.

"Does he now?" I said somewhat surprised. "That's good to hear. But let me ask you something; what are you doing here on your own so far from home?"

He thought for a while before answering, "Well, as I said, Uncle Ike talks a lot about you lot, especially Alfie who he does seem to have a dislike for – almost a fear. Which one of you is Alfie by the way?"

"I'm Alfie," he replied, stepping forward and sticking out his chest.

"Good heavens," gasped Willie. "The way Uncle Ike talks about you, I'd have expected a wild, ferocious animal, but I see you're not."

"No I'm not. I just can't stand bullies, that's all, and that's what your uncle is, a bully!"

"Yes, he is," agreed Willie. "They are all alike. His sons and the Clanton Boys. Both mother and I hate them and wish we could get away. They're just lazy louts. Anyway, to continue, with all the talk of you, I decided to come and see for myself. I actually started out two days ago, meaning to return the same day, but I've been enjoying being on my own – away from the teasing and bullying of my cousins. I suppose I'll be in the bird box when I get home. It's surprising that they haven't sent out a search party by now."

"Yes it is," I said thoughtfully. "Russell, take Jeff and Martin westward and keep a sharp lookout for bandits."

"Aye, aye," shouted Russell as they zoomed skywards.

Turning to Willie I asked, "D'you think you're well enough to travel?"

"Flying's out for a while," came the reply. "But I'll manage a slow walk. Where are you going?"

"To our house where we can get you fit again. It's not too far and besides, I have an idea."

"Are you thinking what I'm thinking?" asked Poppy.

"Probably," I replied. "Come. Let's get going."

Willie did pretty well and we were back home sooner than I thought.

"Everything all right?" asked Dixie, meeting us.

"Yes, thanks Dix," I replied. "We've got him. Willie? Meet Dixie. Dixie's sightless."

"Nice to meet you," said Willie politely. "My uncle Ike speaks highly of you. Says how pretty you are – and he's right. You're beautiful!"

"Why thank you Willie. How nice you are. Harry, what's going to happen to him?" asked Dixie nervously.

"Don't worry Dix, we'll look after him."

CHAPTER 23

THE SHOWDOWN

At that moment, several excited screeches filled the air and, looking up, I saw the crows descending fast.

"Harry! Harry!" they shouted collectively. "They're coming! They're on the way!"

"Slow down lads," I said. "One at a time. Tell me, Russell."

"Okay," he answered. "We spotted them near Lastros, about four k's away and they're definitely looking for something."

"How long before they get here do you think?" I asked.

"A good couple of hours," replied Martin.

"Yes," added Jeff, "they're searching pretty thoroughly, so it'll be at least that."

"The whole gang of them?" asked Poppy.

"We counted six!" answered Russell.

"Six!" shouted Alfie. "There should only be five. Who else has joined them?"

"Oh my gosh," cried Willie. "It can only be my mum!"

"Well that makes sense," said Dixie. "She must be very worried."

"Of course she will be," I agreed. "So let's think for a moment. Martin, you reckon on a couple of hours?"

"Give or take, yes," replied Martin.

"Okay. So that should give us plenty of time to get up there, tell the others all about it, and get ready. Let's go."

"Go?" asked Willie. "Go where?"

"Where, my boy?" I answered. "To the battlefield."

"Eh! H-Harry," stuttered Willie. "What is the battlefield?"

"Well it's a long story," I explained. "But it's to do with your uncle Ike and his gang."

I outlined the plan as we made our way to meet with the others.

"Does this mean there's going to be a fight?" asked a rather shaken Willie.

"Well," I replied, "there may well have been but you turning up may have changed things."

"But what's it got to do with me?" he asked.

"It's got everything to do with you. Don't you see? You're one of their kin, but you're with us."

"You mean I'm a hostage?" he gasped.

"Not really – You're free to go whenever you want, but I hope you stay as you could go a long way to resolving the situation peacefully."

As we approached Angus' place, the quietness was eerie and I began to wonder if the troops were there at all. But as we got closer, I could hear the odd whisper and then became aware of the many eyes that peered out from the foliage. At that moment, our flying squad landed to announce that the enemy was near.

"How close Russell?" I asked.

"About ten minutes' flying time," he replied.

"Okay everybody," I called. "Did you hear that? Ten minutes! Get ready! Alfie, are you in position?"

"Yes Harry," he replied nervously. "I'm good."

"Right! Poppy, Dixie, take cover! Willie? Stand behind me."

And so we waited, holding our breath. Suddenly, there was a great whoosh as the old enemy landed not twenty metres from Alfie.

"Well, well, well!" cackled Ike. "Alfie, so nice to see you."

"Can't say the same about you," replied Alfie defiantly.

And this is where it all went pear shaped when Willie shouted, "Mummy!"

"That's torn it!" whispered Poppy.

"Willie, is that you?" called his frantic mother. "Where are you?"

"Harry!" boomed Ike. "Are you holding our Willie?"

"No, Ike," I responded. "He's not being held. We found him injured and have been taking care of him."

With that, Ike blew up to his full height and screeched at Willie.

"You good for nothing boy!" You've been a pain in the neck ever since your father left. Useless! That's what you are!"

"Come on Ike," said his mother. "He's only a boy."

"You stay out of this!" yelled Ike. "You're just as much a handful. We've never wanted you here! We've put up with you but you've been nothing but a burden!"

"Why you ungrateful miserable old man!" she screamed angrily turning on him. "Why do you think Willie's father left to find us a new home? Because he couldn't stand your unruliness and the dreadful company you keep! And after all we've done for you!"

"What did you ever do for me?" demanded Ike.

"What did I do?" she yelled. "Who do you think keeps your house in order? Without me," she continued, "you'd be living in a pigsty. Well you ruffians can live in a pigsty! I've had it with you!" And with that she flew at him.

I could only stand and stare and all our troops crept out of hiding to watch old Ike taking a beating and beat him she did – clawing him, wings flogging him and her beak tearing out feathers. She was a large bird and old Ike never stood a chance from the sudden onslaught. I couldn't believe her fury. He staggered back.

"Stop woman! Stop!" wailed Ike.

"What?" she screamed. "Stop? I've not started yet!"

And she continued to batter him, feathers flying all over the place until at last she backed off leaving a bruised and bleeding Ike slumped against a tree. There was a collective silence as we all stood there aghast.

Then Freia stepped forward and shouted, "Donnerwetter! Did he deserve that?"

The tension was broken as there was a cheer with voices calling out, "Well done" – "Good for you" – "Bravo." And the troops moved forward to surround the rest of Ike's cowering gang.

"Right you boys, I reckon it's time for you to leave and take what's left of Ike with you. Don't come back! As you can now see, we're more than a match for you."

With their heads hanging, they made their way over to Ike, got him to his feet, and supporting him, flew off. A great cheer went up as they took to the sky and trust Alfie, who gave them one of his raspberries to send them on their way.

"I can't thank you all enough for taking care of my son," said Willie's mother stepping forward. "You've all been so caring."

"It's our pleasure Madame," I said bowing. "What will you do with yourselves now?"

"Oh, we'll go back home and wait for my husband to return. I know he won't be long. Then we'll all be off to start a new life."

"Well," Poppy said, "if you're going home best be careful of Ike."

"Oh, him?" she smiled. "Don't worry about him. He knows what to expect if he misbehaves."

"Yes," agreed Alfie. "We've seen you in action."

Which brought a bout of laughter from us all.

"So," she said, "we'll be on our way. We'll never forget you and will certainly come and visit."

"You're more than welcome Madame," said Dixie. "Russell, maybe you'd like to escort the lady and her son."

"Sure thing Dix," answered Russell. "Come on guys!"

And amid shouts of goodbye and good luck, they were away.

"So 'Arry," said Boubou. "We'll be getting back. Like to be 'ome before dark."

"Of course," I said. "And thanks so much for all your support."

"Tipota," came the answer. "It's nothing!"

And as the Mochlos crowd left for home I called, "See you on the beach real soon!"

That evening, we were all together chattering about the day's exciting events and celebrating a decisive victory. Though strangely enough it was not of our making. More to the point, none of us got hurt, especially Alfie, who could have. So all in all, we couldn't have asked for a more perfect ending.

Suddenly, a happy tune reached our ears.

"What's that sound?" asked Dixie.

And turning around we spotted a lone figure shuffling towards us.

"Good heavens!" said Alfie.

"It can't be," whispered Poppy.

"It is, you know!" I yelled.

"Evening all," smiled Bobby Badger. "Wot's happening?"

THE END